ELO
The Seventh Day
By Leslie

Copyright 2020

Library of Congress Control Number: 2020903740

ISBN: 9798623120090

The boundaries which divide Life from Death are at best shadowy and vague. Who shall say where the one ends, and the other begins?

Edgar Allen Poe

Prologue

Six-year-old Gabriel slid a piece of paper to her father. He sat next to her at the long table in the conference room, the sleazy smile of a used car salesman plastered on his face. The two men on the other side were visibly uncomfortable, squirming in the leather seats and fiddling with papers and pens as they nervously awaited Mr. Murphy's offer. They knew him by reputation, the stories of his shrewd genius having made their way around town for years. Every CEO in Manhattan dreaded the day they had to come to Murphy Equity Group. James Murphy's style was well known. He'd exchange pleasantries, sit quietly for a few moments, then make his offer: the lowest possible amount the seller was willing to take. He somehow always knew and his chipper demeanor made his low-balling all the more insulting.

Mr. Murphy glanced at the note, folded it, and slipped it into his jacket pocket. "Well, Gentlemen, I won't waste your time. My team has crunched the numbers and the best I can do is seven million. I'm sure it's lower than you were hoping, so if you can't accept, no hard feelings." He stood, pulling his daughter's chair out and helping her down. "If you'll excuse me, I have to get this one to school. I'll give you until the end of the day to think it over."

"Wait," one of the men sighed. He stopped, a knowing grin creeping across his face.

"Go wait for me with Mrs. Lee," James whispered to Gabriel, who nodded and left the room. "Yes?"

"We'll take it," the other man said, disappointment and defeat clear in his tone.

"Excellent!" James said, shaking the man's hand. "Let's get those papers signed, shall we?"

In the lobby, Gabriel hovered near the secretary's desk. Mrs. Lee chewed on the end of a pen, the waiting driving her crazy. The doctor should have called by now. What was taking so long?

"Don't worry," Gabriel assured her. "He's fine."

"What?" Mrs. Lee said, just noticing the girl. "Oh, hi, Taran. How are you today?"

"A little sleepy. Daddy got me up early again for his meeting."

"Well, that's no fun. Would you like a pen and some paper to draw with while you wait?"

"No, thanks. I'm not particularly artistic. But he is," she said, pointing to the woman's stomach.

"Who is, sweetie?"

"Daniel. That's what you'll name him, after your husband's dad. He's gonna be a famous painter when he grows up."

The secretary's mouth hung open as she ignored the phone ringing next to her. "How...what?"

"Let's go, Taran," James said, exiting the board room, carrying the signed sales agreement. He placed the papers on the desk and took Gabriel's hand. "Time for school. Kim, take care of these while I'm gone, would you?" The secretary nodded, dazed by the girl's words. Gabriel waved as father and daughter stepped into the elevator, Mrs. Lee slowly raising her hand to wave back. As the elevator doors closed, the phone rang again.

"Murphy Equity Group, how can I direct your call?"

"Is this Mrs. Lee?" the woman on the other end asked.

"Yes."

"Hello, Mrs. Lee, and congratulations! Your suspicions were correct. You're pregnant! We'll need to set up an appointment to determine how far along you are."

She almost dropped the phone. How could the child have known? She hadn't told anyone she thought she might be expecting, not even her husband. And how did she know her father-in-law's name?

"Mrs. Lee?"

"Yes, yes, I'm here." *How did she know?*

"How does it feel, being a *teenager* now?" Gabriel's mother asked, lighting the thirteen candles on the cake that sat in front of her, cloying pink icing spelling out her human name in awkward cursive.

"The same," Gabriel responded, blowing out the candles before her mother was finished.

"You didn't make a wish," Cam said. He was her only friend and the solitary party guest.

"You know there's no point."

"Taran, dear," her mother condescended, her words slurred and her breath reeking of gin. "Don't be so dramatic. A wish is a dream your heart makes. Or is it the other way around?"

"Mother, you're wasted and you're embarrassing me. Can you leave us alone? Please?"

"How dare you speak to me that way?!" Esther shouted. She raised her hand and slapped her daughter hard, causing her mouth to bleed ever so slightly. Cam jumped up from his seat, grasping the cake cutter. Gabriel covered his hand with hers and shook her head. He sat back down. "When your father gets home and he finds out what you said to me--"

"You mean when he gets back from Amber's?" Gabriel shot back. "Oh, I know all about Dad's girlfriend. Well, the chick he pays to bang on weekends. I would have said something, but you already knew. Just didn't want to admit it to yourself. You *should* tell him what I said. You should *also* tell him it's real shitty to miss his only kid's birthday for a cheap fuck."

Esther slapped her again, wishing at that moment that the fall she'd purposefully taken down the stairs when she found out she was pregnant with her had done its job. Gabriel's skin burned hot and her cheeks turned red as she rose from her seat. Without thinking, she used her telekinesis to lift the cake from the table and throw it across the room, sending it smashing into the wall behind her drunk mother. Esther backed away, horror and confusion covering her overly painted face. "What are you?" she all but whispered as she hurried from the room.

That night, James came home to find his wife distraught and more inebriated than usual. She looked terrified and what she'd told him didn't make any sense. He chalked it up to the booze but went up to Taran's room to get her side of the story, anyway. He let himself in, angered at the sight of her smoking a joint, the music from her stereo blaring so loud, he couldn't hear himself yelling at her to turn it down.

"What do you think you're doing?!" he shouted, taking the joint and putting it out with his fingers.

"I'm just trying to calm down," she told him. "Mom was, well, *Mom*, and I--"

"You told her about Amber? How did you know about that?"

"How do I know anything? How do I know *everything*? Don't act surprised. You've been using me for my 'insights' since I was four."

"Taran Ann, there is a difference between work and family. You do not invade people's minds for personal reasons. It's an intrusion."

"It's involuntary."

"Young lady, you will not--"

"Can you go? I need to be alone."

"*Taran Ann Murphy*,"

"Dude, all I can see in my head is a naked blonde from behind and, thanks to you, I know what she feels like on the inside. Please, *get out*." She opened the door behind him without ever leaving her seat on the bed on the other side of the room. James felt his heart jump in his chest. He left the room, his hands trembling, sweat beading on his brow. For the first time, he was afraid of his own daughter.

Fifteen-year-old Gabriel kissed her girlfriend goodnight before falling asleep next to her. Ada's parents had no idea what went on at their sleepovers and Gabriel wasn't sure how long they'd remain oblivious, so she enjoyed it while it lasted, knowing that the strict Catholics would put an end to the relationship if they ever put two and two together. As the girls slept, a man crept into the room. He covered Gabriel's nose and mouth with a rag doused in chloroform, ensuring she'd remain unconscious as he took her from the bed and carried her out of the house.

She woke with a start just as one of her father's security guards was loading her into the back of a town car. She looked behind her, groggy, her head pounding like a drum. Her vision was blurry, but it wasn't hard to make out the house, fully engulfed in flames. "Ada!" she screamed. "ADA!"

A few days later, Gabriel snuck into the city, her best friend by her side, to attend the party of a girl she'd never met, but was said to have the best drugs in Manhattan. While Cam headed to the bathroom to do a bump, Gabriel floated on a heroin cloud, blissful nothing replacing the constant barrage of other people's thoughts in her mind. She fell back into the couch, allowing the fog to carry her away. It was the closest thing to Heaven she'd felt since before she was born.

As she lay there, she suddenly felt something familiar; a knowing. A longing. A pull in a particular direction. It was one of them. She glanced around, her eyes eventually falling to a boy about her age, beer in one hand, a girl's waist in the other. He was tall with dark hair and a no-fucks-given attitude. She recognized him immediately. "Barachiel," she whispered. She giggled, unable to muster the energy or gumption to get up and speak to him. He walked off, taking his girlfriend into a bedroom and closing the door.

"Heroin, really?" Cam lectured. "You know how addictive that shit is?"

"It makes the voices disappear," Gabriel explained. "Shh."

"I know you're messed up about Ada, but this is too much."

"I said, 'shh'."

"You can't ignore what happened forever. You're gonna have to deal with it, preferably before you OD."

"It just hurts too much right now. I'll talk about it when I can go five sober minutes without wanting to hurt someone."

"All right, let's get you home before someone calls the cops on this party." He picked her up and threw her over his shoulder, carrying her from the apartment and to the elevator.

"My pal, Cam. Always taking care of me."

"Somebody's got to."

The two arrived back at Gabriel's house just after three in the morning, the drive from Manhattan to Fairfield taking about an hour and a half. They were greeted by a gun in their faces, James thinking he'd heard an intruder.

"Taran, what were you doing out so late?" he barked, putting the gun down.

"Since when do you have a gun of your own?" Gabriel wondered. "Where are your security bros?"

"They're off for the night. Where were you?"

"Probably fornicating with that boy," her mother slurred from the top of the stairs.

Gabriel laughed. "Dude, gross," she snickered as Cam helped her up the steps.

"That's not something you have to worry about, ma'am," Cam assured Esther, taking note of the gin and tonic in her hand.

"You keep acting this way, you'll end up pregnant," Esther warned.

"Guess again," Gabriel chuckled.

"Why not? Because you're an abomination?"

"What?"

"We know about that girl," Esther spat.

"Esther!" James cautioned from the foyer.

"Oh, I already know," Gabriel told them. "I know you killed her, and her parents, and her fucking dog, you pieces of shit. Dad had his goons burn her fucking house down and made it look like an electrical fire because you couldn't stand the thought of your country club buddies finding out you had a gay daughter. How *embarrassing* that would have been for you. Did you honestly think I didn't know? Why do you think I've been stoned out of my gourd all week? Or were you too busy banging hookers and hiding in a bottle to notice?"

Esther dropped her glass and threw her hands into her daughter's chest, sending her flailing backward and down the marble staircase, her anger getting the better of her.

Cam watched in horror as Gabriel's neck snapped, her limp body hitting the floor, blood gushing from her head at her father's feet.

"Oh, my God!" James gasped.

Cam's rage overtook him, the world around him going black. He grabbed Esther by the hair and slammed her head into the banister, over and over, until there was nothing left but a mangled lump of unrecognizable flesh where her face used to be. James shot up at the boy, but he barreled down the steps, unfazed, the bullets hitting his chest seeming to have no effect. When he reached the last step, Gabriel stood, rubbing her neck as it put itself back in proper alignment.

"That was rude," she muttered.

James clutched his chest. "What the hell are you?"

"You wouldn't believe me."

"You're possessed!" he blurted. "You're a demon!"

"Wow."

"It's the only thing that makes sense. You're a monster!"

"I'm not a monster," she snapped.

"Demon!" he shouted, shooting Gabriel in the heart. She fell, dying at the hands of her parents for a second time. Cam's eyes became slits and his blood pressure rose. He punched James, breaking his nose before gripping the sides of his head and spinning it around, snapping his neck. As the man's body fell, Cam's mind cleared. He got his breathing under control and wiped the blood from his hands onto his jeans.

"Gabriel," he said, trying to gently shake her awake. "Gabriel, you okay?"

"I'm fine," she grunted, getting to her feet. "It'll take a lot more than a couple of fucked up parents to kill this bitch."

"I'm sorry. I lost it," he admitted as she looked over her dead parents' bodies.

"Yeah, you did. It'll be fine. I'll clean up, change clothes, tell them I was asleep and heard gunshots, woke up, and found this. You have to go, though."

"I don't want to leave you alone."

"I'm all right, I swear."

"But, your parents--"

"It doesn't matter."

"G, are you sure?"

"You'd be a suspect."

"But--"

"Camael, please. Go home."

"All right," he said, giving her a quick hug before opening the door to leave. "Love you, sis."

"Love you, too." She closed the door behind him and leaned against it, looking down at her shirt and around the room. "What a mess."

Chapter 1

Wyatt stood over his son's fresh grave, his face sullen and his body numb. He hadn't eaten or slept in the last two days, the pain in his gut replacing all other sensations. He felt no fatigue or hunger. He was oblivious to all manner of discomfort, including the heat of the summer sun beating down on him as he stood, alone, tears blurring the words on the headstones. His wife and his son, buried not far from his parents, all dead because of him, in one way or another. Guilt, grief, and rage mingled in his chest as he tried to maintain an upright position, a feat that proved more difficult by the second.

"You should go over there," Valerie told Gabriel as the two watched their brother from behind a tree a few yards away.

"He doesn't want to see me," Gabriel said. "The whole 'sending-Michelle-to-spy' thing. I'm gonna give him some space. You should talk to him, though. Keep an eye. He shouldn't be alone."

"He's gotta be devastated."

"He is." She wiped away a tear as she observed him, his misery overwhelming, even at a distance, and her own feelings of loss proving difficult to manage.

"Girl, are you *crying*?" Valerie asked.

"I'm not made of stone."

"All right, but this is the second time I've ever seen you cry *in my life.*"

"Just because he was fucked up, doesn't mean I didn't care about him. He *was* our nephew. I loved that kid."

"Well, damn, if you're over here shedding tears, Wyatt's gotta be--"

"Broken," Gabriel said, her voice shaky. "He's completely destroyed. I have a plane to catch, but you should talk to him."

"You have a *what*? *Now?*"

"Girl, I've got so many balls in the air, I could join the circus. Don't leave him alone." Gabriel walked back to her car, texting Allydia once she was inside. *As soon as the sun goes down, you get your fangy ass to Wyatt's dad's place. Do not let him be alone. Not for a second.*

"How are you holding up?" Valerie asked, rubbing Wyatt's arm as she stood next to him.

"Not well," he grumbled.

"I'm so sorry. Is there anything I can do?"

"Unlikely."

"You know I'm here if you feel like talking."

"I know." He looked up from the headstone. "Gabriel didn't show?"

"She was here. Said you didn't want to see her."

"She's not wrong."

"Hey, you wanna come over for dinner tonight? Malik can make anything you want."

"No, thanks."

"Maybe I'll just bring you something, then."

"Don't," he ordered. "I want to be alone."

"I feel like that's a bad idea. Gabriel said--"

"I couldn't care less what Gabriel said. *She's not here.* She's probably with Lucifer at her place, celebrating."

"Man, that girl was crying. Her. *Crying.* She might not have many emotions, but she loved Will, too. Maybe don't be so hard on her."

Wyatt sighed. "Fine. Where is she? Home?"

"No, she said she had a plane to catch. You should call her, though. No sense pushing her away when you need your family most."

"A plane?" he asked. "To where?"

"Beats me."

"Huh." His expression turned from that of despair to angry determination. "Interesting."

"Boy, what are you thinking?"

He glared down at her, the look on his face making the hairs on the back of her neck stand up. "Don't get in my way."

11

The door to Gabriel's apartment flew open, Wyatt having kicked it in. He had a key, but not the patience for using it. Lucifer stood from his spot on the couch, setting his book on the end table.

"Brother," he greeted. "Apologies for missing the funeral. I assumed my presence there would have been in bad taste."

Without a word, Wyatt hurled a bolt of lightning into the devil's chest, sending him flying back into the sofa, smoke rising from the seared flesh now exposed by the hole burned in his button-down.

"That smarts," Lucifer complained, setting himself up.

"Wyatt, stop!" Valerie yelped, running in behind him as he marched toward Lucifer, unable or unwilling to hear her. "Wyatt!"

He threw a ball of electricity into his brother's chest, then another. Lucifer winced but didn't fight back. "It's all right, sister," he said, raising a hand to keep her back. "We all know I deserve it."

Wyatt leaped over the ottoman and wrapped his hands around his brother's neck, squeezing so hard, his nails drew blood. He then unleashed all the power he could muster, taking it from every source in the apartment, causing lights to shatter and appliances to explode. Lucifer's eyes bulged and his nose spewed blood as his body shook violently, his mouth foaming.

"Wyatt, stop!" Valerie pleaded. "You're killing him!"

"That's the goal," Wyatt grunted, the look in his eyes that of a rabid dog.

Her heart racing, Valerie grabbed the sides of Wyatt's head and showed him his own memory, revealing to him what had actually happened the night his son died. He saw it all; his conversation with Lucifer in the woods, holding Will under the rushing water of the creek. He could feel the boy thrashing in the water, then going limp. He watched as his soul drifted away. He remembered instructing his brother to tell him what he'd done and returning to his body, recreating its organs and structure. He even remembered the affection he, as Barachiel, had for Lucifer, his older but damaged and somewhat needy brother, that he'd missed terribly since the last time they'd been together.

Valerie let go and backed away as Wyatt stumbled, collapsing onto the ottoman, short of breath and eyes wide.

Lucifer healed and jolted up. "Why did you do that?!" he barked at his sister. "Those memories were meant to stay buried!"

"Uh, *you're welcome*," she snapped.

"The blame should have been mine to bear."

"Are you stupid? He was *killing you*."

"I would have been fine. Besides, look at him now. He can't handle the burden of what he's done! He's much too fragile. *We went over this.*"

"I couldn't just stand here and let him--" She stopped as Wyatt got up and staggered toward the door. "Where you goin'?"

He walked to the hall, not looking back. "Leave me alone."

Wyatt rifled through his father's desk, falling into the chair when he found what he'd been looking for. He opened the bottle of scotch and guzzled the contents, ignoring the empty glass that sat in front of him. The study was dim and dust had begun to collect on the globe in the corner next to the shaded window. The room itself felt lost, serving no purpose since the passing of its former occupant, another loss Wyatt still hadn't fully dealt with. When the bottle was empty, he searched for another, tossing papers and books from the desk drawers before throwing the lamp, shattering it against the wall, and heaving the desk from its place to the other side of the room, blocking the doorway. He fell to the floor and sobbed, his chest tight and heavy as he trembled, his wailing piquing the interest of the ghost that resided there. She lurked in the far corner, kneeling and folding her hands as she watched him, curious. She hoped that he would stay. She'd missed him.

Chapter 2

In life, Margaret had been an immigrant to this city. Having left Ireland in the hopes of a better life, she quickly learned that New York was no place for a young woman on her own. Luckily, she'd been taken in by The Whyos who gave her food and proper clothes. They'd even found a job for her working as a maid for a prominent businessman. He'd recently rented an apartment in a newly constructed building in a remote part of town and wanted to keep it in pristine condition, even though he had no intention of actually living there. She stayed in the servant's quarters: a tiny room with one window, a mattress on the floor, and not much else. It was small, but so was she, standing five feet exactly and weighing about ninety pounds. Other people may have seen her room as cramped or inadequate, but it was warm and dry with a beautiful view. As a poor, illiterate farmer's daughter who'd grown up fighting for scraps, never having owned a pair of shoes until she'd been given refuge in The Bowery, servant's quarters seemed like a luxury.

She'd been washing the windows when the man made his first appearance. Until then, she'd never actually met her employer. Once a week for two months, he'd leave her payment on the desk in the study. She'd never seen his face. She didn't even know his name.

He'd ignored her at first, busy with some sort of paperwork. She had curtsied when he entered the room, but she was sure he hadn't noticed. She continued with her work, leaving the man to his, assuming it must be important. He'd spent all day in the study, looking over papers, occasionally scribbling something on one of them. She'd made sure to stay quiet, not wanting to break his concentration. She'd heard horror stories of abusive employers, beating their servants with belts or even whips for minor infractions. One girl that worked as a nanny in the building had several marks on her arms; burns from her master's cigars. She had been lucky, the girl had told her, that her boss was never around. Now that he was, she couldn't help but be nervous. Still, the sun was setting and it was time for her to retire for the evening. She couldn't just do that, though. She knew the protocol. She had to ask permission. So, she made her way to the study, her heart racing and her throat going dry.

The door had been left ajar. She gently tapped on it before entering, keeping her eyes on the floor. "Excuse me, sir." She curtsied again.

He looked up from his mound of paperwork. "Yes?"

"I've finished for the day, sir. Is there anything else you need?"

"Stand up straight, girl. Let me get a look at you."

She did as she was told.

"You're a pretty little thing, aren't you?"

"If you say so, sir."

"I absolutely do. How old are you?"

"I turned eighteen last month, sir."

"Very good. Tell me, can you read?"

She was embarrassed to answer but choked back her pride. "No, sir."

"Ah. Well, then, I suppose I'll have to teach you. Come, sit."

"Yes, sir." She sat in the chair across from the desk, but he shook his head.

"No, girl. *Here*." He patted his knee. She swallowed hard and did her best not to show how uncomfortable it made her as she went around the desk and sat on his leg. "First, you'll have to learn what the letters are. See this right here?" he pointed to a mark on a page from the pile.

She nodded.

"That's 'A'. This one here, that's 'B'. Do you know the sounds they make?"

She shook her head.

"That's fine. You'll get there. Now, this letter is 'C'. This here is 'D'."

She looked at the marks as he pointed them out, trying to memorize them. She didn't know why he wanted her to become literate. Most employers didn't care, so she'd been told. Some even preferred their staff to be unable to read. Less chance of them moving on to better jobs and leaving them in the lurch. Plus, reading a book could make a person lose track of time, time that would be better spent working. But, if he needed her to read, she would learn. Anything to keep her position.

As he spoke, the low, soothing sound of his voice distracted her. She snuck a look at him, noticing the way his eyes sparkled, green as the grass back home. He was older, at least forty, but handsome with wisps of gray running through his otherwise deep chestnut hair. He smelled of cedar and tobacco and his leg felt warm underneath her. His left hand was firmly placed on the small of her back, presumably to keep her steady. But, as he went through the alphabet, that hand began to lower, brushing over and then settling on her backside.

She knew that was inappropriate but as anxious as it made her, there was part of her that didn't mind. It felt nice to be getting attention from a man, even if it was her boss. No man had looked at her twice since she'd arrived in this country, and this was a fine man, indeed. She wondered if she could ingratiate herself to him. Seduce him, even. If she could find a way to make him fall in love with her, maybe he would marry her. She could live a life of luxury and opulence instead that of a poor maid. *Fairytales*, she thought as she pushed the daydream aside and tried to focus. She concentrated on the marks on the page, following his words as best she could. But, as he spoke, his voice became fainter. She could feel his breath on her cheek, warm against her skin. He went quiet, his right hand moving from the papers to her leg.

He pulled up her skirt and petticoat, slowly as to gauge her response. She allowed it. He slid his hand up, gliding over and between her legs as he nuzzled her neck. She fluttered with anticipation, wanting to behave demurely, but aching for his touch. He gently pushed her legs apart, just enough that he could slip his fingers inside. Her breathing quickened as he messaged her. She could feel her body responding to him, unable to control the movements of her hips. She threw her arm around his shoulders to balance herself. He took that as an invitation to take things to the next level.

He hoisted her onto the desk, carefully pushing his papers to the side. He pushed up her clothes, revealing her pale, freckled skin. He hastily removed his trousers and pulled her to the edge of the desk, opening her legs and thrusting himself into her. She gasped, the combination of pain and pleasure flooding through her. He grasped her rear, squeezing as he continued. She lay back, grinding against him, her hands over her head holding on to the desk for stability. She bit her lip, stifling the cries that begged to escape her lips. She'd never felt anything like this. Was this what an orgasm felt like? She'd never had one but had been informed by the other servant girls in the building that they *were* possible. The boys she'd been with back in Ireland had been so quick to finish, it was hardly pleasurable for her at all. Now, though, her skin felt hot, like bathwater washing over her. Wave after wave of euphoria gripped her as she held on to the desk, her knuckles going white. He continued to buck, pushing hard and fast into her. She was sure she'd have bruises where his fingers dug into her behind, but she didn't care. She exploded with pleasure, every part of her tingling. Finally, the man grunted, his face twisting as sweat ran down his temples. His face had gone red and he trembled as he filled her.

When he was done, he put his pants back on and wiped the sweat from his brow. He didn't look at her. He gathered his papers and walked toward the door. "That's all for today." He left the apartment, leaving Margaret in a state of shame. She slid off of the desk, standing and adjusting her dress, her legs weak. It had been a ruse. The man had had no interest in teaching her to read. It was an excuse to get her close.

"I'm so stupid," she whimpered, holding back the tears that threatened to fall. She refused to let them. "It's all right," she told herself. "I'm fine."

But she wasn't, and she could feel in her gut that she would never be fine again.

Months had passed. By the time the man returned, Margaret had begun to show. She had tried to hide her

17

condition with an oversized uniform, but there was no disguising her bump given her small frame.

She'd curtsied as he entered the apartment, keeping her eyes averted. He paused to look her over before heading to the study, this time closing the door. She let out a sigh of relief. She knew she'd have to tell him. She'd have to do it today. It could be *another* six months or more before she'd see him again. Her heart thumped in her chest as she awaited the conversation, unsure of what exactly she'd say. She didn't want to sound bitter, though she was still angry with him for using her the way he had. She wanted to appear strong, capable of handling this on her own if that's what he wanted. He would *not* get the best of her. He would *not* see her cry.

As the sun set, he finally exited the study, a stern look sharpening his features. She turned to face him and curtsied again. Before she could say a word, he took her hand and thrust fifty dollars into it.

"Sir?"

"There's a man in Syracuse, a doctor," he told her. "His method is less painful, I've heard. Safer."

"I don't understand, sir."

"I believe that you do." He glanced down at her belly.

She was horrified. "You want me to--"

"I'm a married man, girl. My wife has given me six children and while I may indulge in the occasional indiscretion, I will not shame her by fathering a bastard with *the help*. You *will* see the doctor. I trust you'll be discreet." And with that, he took his leave.

She stood there, mouth agape and head spinning. What he was asking was impossible. She was too far along. She'd felt the quickening. To end the pregnancy now would be a sin. She couldn't do what he'd demanded. She simply couldn't.

Two months later, the man returned. She shuddered at the fire in his eyes, his face red with rage.

"You defied my orders!" he bellowed.

"I'm sorry, sir. It was too late. I couldn't--"

"I don't want to hear your excuses! You have no idea what you've done!" He paced the floor as she cowered in the corner, hands folded, bracing herself for the beating she was sure she was about to receive.

"I haven't spent the money. I left it in your desk. I don't want anything from you."

"It's not about the money, you stupid girl!" He bounded toward her, his face twisted in anger. She could see that he wanted to hit her. She recognized the look. Her father used to look at her mother like that just before he'd start in. He didn't do it, though. Instead, he disappeared into another room. When he came back, he was carrying a toolbox. Sweat beaded on his forehead and his face had gone pale, the look of a man who knew he was about to do something truly horrific.

He left, slamming the door behind him. She was stunned. She'd been sure he'd reprimand her in some way. When no punishment was allocated, she breathed a sigh of relief. He was angry, yes, and she'd have to raise her baby alone. She would have to concoct a story of a fake husband. Maybe a Marine, killed in the Rebellion in Hawaii. It would be difficult, but it was doable. She would find a way. She would have her baby and she would show him the love she'd never known herself.

She'd been so lost in her own thoughts, she hadn't heard the pounding. It was coming from the door. She thought the man had come back. Perhaps he'd left his key in his rush to get out of there. She went to answer, but the door wouldn't open. The knob turned, but it wouldn't pull to. She pulled harder. Nothing. She kept pulling, but it wouldn't budge.

"Sir?" she called. "Sir, the door's stuck!"

No answer. Just more pounding.

"Sir? Sir?!"

Again, no answer. The pounding stopped.

"Sir, I can't open the door!" She smacked her hand against it a few times, hoping he'd be able to hear her now that he'd stopped knocking himself. "Sir!" She hit the door a few more times, confusion giving way to panic. She stepped back, catching her breath.

19

Her hands shook and her eyes became saucers as she realized what had happened. He hadn't been knocking. He'd been nailing the door shut. He'd trapped her inside.

She threw herself at the door, screaming and banging her fists against the wood. "HELP! HELP ME, PLEASE!" But no one came.

There was no food in the apartment. She was sure she would starve. But, it was worse than that. The next day when she awoke, she discovered the water had been shut off. She would be dead inside of a week with no water. He had done it purposefully. He was trying to kill her.

She should have been afraid. She wasn't. She was enraged. She drank the water from toilet tanks and convinced herself she'd survive on spite alone. He'd have to come back eventually. The smell of a rotting corpse would surely draw suspicion. He'd have to dispose of her body. So, when he came back, she'd have her revenge. She slept with a kitchen knife under her pillow and waited.

Another week had gone by. She'd run out of water and she hadn't felt her baby move in two days. She'd noticed the blood before she'd felt any pain.

On her mattress in the servant's quarters, she gave birth to her son. His skin was gray and his body limp. He never cried, but she did. For three days, she held her bundle and sobbed. She was hot with fever and would soon join her boy in death. It was her only consolation. She would forever hold her baby in her arms.

On the fourth night, the man returned. Dropping his toolbox at the sight of the dead child. He covered his mouth and sank to his knees.

"You did this to us," she spat, her voice barely audible. "I will tell everyone what you've done. I will--"

"You'll tell no one." He growled, pinning her to the blood-soaked bed. He sat on her chest, holding her arms down with his legs. The knife peeked out from under the pillow. He took it and grasped her jaw, holding her mouth open. She tried to bite him, but he persisted in overpowering her, not a difficult feat, considering. He couldn't get a proper grip on her tongue, so instead of a clean cut, he hacked at it, mutilating it, sending bits of tissue flying in all directions. "You won't tell a soul. If only you could write."

She screamed in pain, blood gurgling in her throat and pouring out her mouth. Even when he stood, she couldn't move. Between infection and blood loss, she was too weak. Her vision became blurry, but as she faded, she saw the man take a tool from his box and begin to pry up a floorboard.

When she woke, the man was hammering a nail into the floor. She looked around wildly, digging through the sheets. Where was he? Where was her son? She pleaded with her eyes, but the man just gathered his tools. He grabbed her by the arm and started to drag her from the room. She yanked on his coat and pointed to the bed as they left.

"The child?" he mocked.

She nodded.

"He's where no one will ever find him."

Her eyes darted back to the room, then up at him. *Holy God*, she thought. *He's put him in the floor.*

It was late, just after two in the morning. The entire building was asleep. She tried to scream as he carried her from the apartment to the elevator, but her voice was faint. She tried to claw at him, but her hands were numb. She didn't make a scratch. Once outside, he raced to the park across the way, nearly dropping her as he hurried. He found a wooded area and set her on her feet. She couldn't stand on her own and tried to balance herself by holding on to his shoulder, but he pushed her away. She fell to the cold ground, the light snow stinging her exposed skin like a thousand tiny needles. He walked off, never looking back.

She tried to crawl to the street, but she was so far gone, it may as well have been a million miles away. She collapsed, the exhaustion overwhelming her. She drifted off and as she pictured her son's tiny face one more time, a single tear fell to her cheek. *At least he never saw me cry.*

Suddenly, she was back in the apartment. It had changed, having been remodeled. Everything was different. She'd tried to go back to the servant's quarters, to find her baby, but the room was gone. It was now part of a parlor decorated in strange furniture and inhabited by people she didn't recognize. There was a man, a lawyer from what she gathered, having listened in on his conversations, and his very pregnant wife. They were happy. It was nice. But, it was immediately clear to her that they couldn't see her, which could only mean that she had died in the park that night and was now haunting this place as a ghoul. She grew depressed, spending all of her time crying over her baby's wooden grave and stalking the mother-to-be, who she could tell was beginning to be impacted emotionally by her presence, but what could she do? She couldn't leave. Not without her son.

As her depression grew, so did the woman's. She began behaving erratically. Margaret knew she was adversely affecting her, so she maintained a distance, keeping to the corners and staying quiet. Not that she could speak if she'd wanted to. Not without her tongue.

Soon, the day came when the lawyer brought his new son home. He was perfect with dark hair and eyes and a sweet disposition. She fell in love with the boy, watching as nannies and maids cared for him. The mother hadn't returned from the hospital and the father became more and more absent as the boy grew. She decided he'd be hers, a replacement for the child so cruelly taken from her. She spent years watching over him, taking pride in his accomplishments and joy in his sweet smile.

The years passed, though, and the boy grew into a man. It wasn't long before the ache of losing her own son returned and she again cried for him. She thought she would suffer alone for eternity, until one night, the boy called Wyatt heard her.

She tried to get his attention, to tell him what had happened. If she could just see her baby, hold him one more time, maybe she could move on. But, the boy went away, shipped off to college by his father who meant well but was very clearly not equipped to handle the job of 'parent'. But, then, a Christmas miracle. The boy had returned. When she was sure the father was asleep, she snuck into Wyatt's room and grunted at him until he woke. Still half unconscious, he'd sprung up from his bed and rushed to follow her to the spot. She'd pointed to it and he'd begun working, trying his damnedest to pull up the boards. The lawyer caught him, though, and that was the end of that.

    She couldn't say that she'd been sorry to see the lawyer die. He'd reminded her of the man that murdered her and stole her baby in that he was a workaholic, cold, and seemed to lack empathy. But, as she watched Wyatt, the boy she'd adopted in her heart, now a man with a broken spirit mourn what she assumed to be the loss of his father, she couldn't help but mourn with him. Maybe she'd misjudged the lawyer. Either way, she still had a soft spot for the man before her. The boy she'd thought of as her own.

Chapter 3

Gabriel stared through the window of Mitchell Spade's suburban Virginia McMansion. The man sat in a high-backed chair in his home office, his messy desk littered with files. He was talking on the phone, too quietly for Gabriel to hear through the glass. She flicked her wrist, attempting to snap his neck. Nothing happened. She waved at the desk, trying to set it on fire. Nothing. It was as she'd suspected; he was invulnerable. Lilith had placed a protection spell on him, rendering her powers useless. "Well, that frosts my cookies," she muttered, turning to leave. It had been a long shot, but she'd hoped Lilith had neglected to insulate her general from supernatural threats. It would have been so much easier, just a quick motion of her hand and the whole thing would have been over. The lives that could have been saved, not to mention the time she could have spent keeping an eye on her grieving brother, making sure he didn't do anything crazy. Now, she'd have to rely on the others to watch over him and *none of them* were equipped.

I know it's daytime, but I have a bad feeling, Gabriel texted. *Get your ass up and get to Wyatt's NOW.* She sat, shifting in her aisle seat as the plane made its way to the city. It was only a little more than an hour flight, so she'd decided to fly commercial. Judging by the turbulence, that had been a mistake. The flight attendant, a pretty blonde with a chipper smile, made the usual 'everything's fine' announcement and instructed the passengers to fasten their seat belts. Gabriel took note of how attractive she was and was thinking about striking up a conversation once the plane landed when she was jolted forward. The plane shook violently. A bird had flown into one of the engines and the pilot was unable to compensate. Oxygen masks dropped and she could feel the other passengers panic as they scrambled to put them on, screaming and texting goodbyes to their loved ones. They were falling fast, a crash inevitable. Just as Gabriel was about to use her telekinesis to hold the plane up, she saw the flight attendant raising her hands to her shoulders. She was whispering something Gabriel couldn't make out from that distance; a chant? The plane slowly corrected itself as the woman muttered under her breath. "What fresh hell?" Gabriel said to herself.

"Attention passengers," the pilot's voice murmured over the intercom. "We're experiencing some technical difficulties and will be making an emergency landing in Harrisburg for repairs." Gabriel couldn't hear the rest of his announcement over the moans of derision from the other passengers. *So ungrateful,* she thought.

She waited until the other passengers had all deplaned before approaching the flight attendant. She was surprised when she got close that she couldn't hear her thoughts. She tried to look inside her mind, but all she saw was the face of another woman, yelling at her to 'get out'.

"Was that Violet?" she wondered allowed.

The flight attendant's face went pale. "Excuse me?"

"In your head. That was Violet, right? Tituba's daughter? Wow. I thought her line died out *years* ago."

"I don't know what you're--"

"It's okay," Gabriel assured her. "I won't tell anyone. I was just coming to see how you saved the plane, but that question's been answered, hasn't it? You're a witch. A *powerful* witch. Descendant of Tituba Indian. I'm not often impressed, but--"

The flight attendant looked around nervously. "How did you know that?"

"I'm not exactly 'normal'. What are you doing right now? You wanna get some dinner? Looks like we're stuck here for a while. I've never actually been to Pennsylvania. What's there to eat around here? I'm starving."

"Um,"

"I'm Gabriel."

"Wendy."

"It's nice to meet you, Wendy. Anyone tell you lately how gorgeous you are? Like, *stunning.*"

"Thanks," she tucked her hair behind her ear as they left the plane. "How did you--"

"We'll talk about it later, maybe someplace less people-y. You hungry?"

"Usually." Wendy blushed, a rush of excitement running through her as Gabriel brushed the hair off her shoulder, her touch electric.

"Let's go, then."

"You're hitting on me, right? I have a hard time distinguishing flirting from people just being nice."

Gabriel smiled. "Oh, I'm *definitely* hitting on you."

Chapter 4

As the tub filled, Wyatt took a swig from a freshly opened bottle of whisky he'd found in his father's pantry. He slipped off his shoes and his jacket before climbing in, not bothering to turn the faucet off. The water was cold and sent chills all through his body as he lay himself down, the icy pool covering his face. He looked up at the ceiling, then closed his eyes, opening his mouth and inhaling the frosty liquid. It felt like needles in his lungs, stinging and sharp as he seized. The pain was intense but soon was over, replaced by quiet nothing.

"Wyatt?" Allydia called from the front door. She let herself in and took off her cloak. The sun wasn't quite down, but Gabriel's incessant texting had woken her. Any other time, her phone would have been off while she slept, but with her lover being in such a fragile state, she couldn't risk it. She had to make herself available to him any time of the night *or* day. "Wyatt?" She followed the sound of water running and entered the bathroom, horrified at the sight of his lifeless body in the tub. "WYATT!" She pulled him from water that overflowed to the tile floor. She pounded on his chest until he sprung up, hacking up fluid and gasping for air. "Why would you do this?" she cried, turning off the faucet.

"Leave me alone, Allydia," he commanded, taking the whisky from the vanity and gulping it down as he sat in the inch of water that now covered the floor.

"I won't. Your sister was right, you are not to be left to your own devices."

"My sister," he scoffed. "*Of course* she sent you. I don't need a babysitter."

"I beg to differ."

"I'm fine."

"You just tried to kill yourself! You aren't in the same *hemisphere* as '*fine*'."

"It's not like I'll *stay* dead," he asserted, drinking the last of the whisky.

"You need help. Let me be of assistance."

"There's nothing you can do. My father's dead and I killed my son. I don't deserve saving. You should have left me where I was."

"What are you saying? *Lucifer--*"

"Took the fall," he interrupted, trembling with rage and guilt as he spoke. "*I killed Will. I remember it. I can still feel my hands on his neck, holding him under until he stopped moving. I'm* the monster. Lucifer tried to *protect* me. He didn't want me to know what I'd done when I was *him*, this *thing* inside. This *angel*."

"Barachiel," she realized.

"Just go."

"Wyatt,"

He smashed the bottle on the side of the tub and held the jagged edge to his wrist, slicing it open.

"Wyatt!" She jumped back, the scent of his blood causing her eyes to dilate and her heart to race.

"Get out!"

She backed out of the room, running from the apartment, afraid of what she'd do, the intoxicating aroma of his blood calling her to drink him dry. She phoned Gabriel, but no answer. She knew Lucifer would be of no help in this situation, so she called the only person left.

"Hello," Valerie answered.

"Valerie, hello. Gabriel gave me your number in case of an emergency and I'd say your brother repeatedly committing suicide in his bathroom counts as such, yes?"

"Holy shit! I'm on my way."

Valerie entered the dark apartment, fumbling around for a light switch. She'd never actually been to Wyatt's place before and at first glance, it seemed typical of a stuffy old white guy, which his father had been. She passed the bookshelves, stereo, and television, noticing how archaic they seemed. Who had a stereo anymore? She found Wyatt in the kitchen, sitting on the island, drinking scotch straight from the bottle, his clothes wet and his sleeve covered in blood.

"I'm finding them everywhere," he slurred, holding up the bottle. "In cabinets and dresser drawers. I found a flask in the *couch cushions*. I didn't know he had that big of a problem."

"Your girlfriend called," Valerie said, hopping up to sit next to him. "You have any idea how un-fucking-nerving it is to have a *vampire* call you saying your brother's *killing himself?*"

"She shouldn't have bothered you."

"I'm not bothered. I'm *angry*. What the fuck do you think you're doin'?"

"Don't lecture me."

"I'm not saying don't be fucked up," she made clear. "It's a fucked up situation and I can't even imagine what you're going through, but repetitive suicide? You know that is not okay."

"Leave me alone."

"That is *not* happening."

"Go!"

"Boy, don't yell at *me*. Your girlfriend might put up with that shit, but *I* won't."

"Sorry."

"You're exhausted. Go put on some dry clothes and go to bed. I'll be here when you get up."

"You don't have to--"

"I've lost one brother. I won't lose another one, you hear me?"

Wyatt sighed and put the whisky on the counter before heading off to his childhood bedroom.

"Love you!" she called after him. "I'll be checking in on you periodically to make sure you're still breathing, so don't lock that fucking door!"

Chapter 5

"So, what are you, psychic?" Wendy asked as she and Gabriel sat down in the back booth of the restaurant, out of earshot of the other patrons.

"Sort of. I'm telepathic, empathetic, telekinetic, and pyrokinetic."

"*Pyro*kinetic? I didn't know that was a real thing."

Gabriel took a bite of bread. "It's pretty rare."

"So, you can *literally* set stuff on fire?"

"Yeah. It's not that interesting. Tell me about *you*. Why did I think the Tituban line was extinct?"

"It mostly is." She took a piece of bread from the basket and smoothed on a pat of butter. "After World War Two, a lot of guys came back still in a combative headspace. With no more Nazis to fight, a group of dudes targeted witches. My grandmother's coven was wiped out. She and her sister were the only ones that got away. They left Tarrytown, moved to New York. They figured a city that big would be a good place to hide, get lost in a sea of people. My grandmother eventually moved back and that's where I grew up."

"And Violet in your head?"

"Before she died, my grandmother used one of Violet's protection spells to keep other witches from reading my thoughts. She was afraid of them getting hold of our spells, stealing our magic. It's too powerful for most witches. They can't handle it. It corrupts them, makes them violent and power-hungry."

"Wow. So, it's just you left?"

"Me and my great-aunt, but I've never met her. She and my grandma had a fight in the fifties about what they should do with their magic. Grandma wanted to keep it in the bloodline. Grace couldn't have kids, so she wanted to start a new coven and share her power so it wouldn't die with her. Standard family feud."

Gabriel laughed. "Yeah, totally normal."

Wendy smiled. "What's *your* family like?"

"Big, complicated. Kinda dark."

She laughed. "So, brothers and sisters?"

"Tons."

"Parents?"

"Died when I was in high school."

"Oh, sorry."

"Don't be. I'm not."

"I feel like that should freak me out, but it doesn't."

They both laughed. They chatted for several minutes, unable to take their eyes off each other even to order. They barely noticed when the food came as their flirtation continued. Gabriel sipped her soda while Wendy finally cut into her steak, her face falling in disappointment.

"What's wrong?"

"It's fine," Wendy accepted. "I ordered medium. It's rare. It's not a big deal."

Gabriel looked around to make sure no one could see them and slid Wendy's plate to her side of the table. She covered the steak with her hand, a flame appearing between them, cooking the meat to temperature like a broiler. The fire dissipated and she slid the plate back.

Wendy was clearly impressed. "That was damn sexy."

Gabriel gleaned. "I'm a sexy bitch."

She giggled. "You really are. You wanna get a hotel room after this?"

She showed her the confirmation screen on her phone. "Girl, I already booked one."

When dinner was over, they took a cab to the hotel. As they traveled, they let their hands wander up one another's thighs. Feeling frisky, Gabriel glided her hand underneath the skirt of Wendy's flight attendant's uniform and slid her fingers between her soft cotton panties and her skin.

She touched her arm and whispered, "What if he sees?"

Gabriel glanced at the driver and back at her. "I'm making sure he keeps his eyes on the road. Telekinetic, remember?"

"Oh, we're gonna have *all kinds* of fun together." She kissed her softly and opened her legs, pulling her closer. Gabriel continued to touch her until they reached their destination. Once in their room, the kissing became more intense. They kicked off their shoes and stumbled to the bed.

Gabriel slipped off Wendy's panties and pushed up her skirt, beginning the marathon lovemaking session that ran into the early morning hours.

"I've never done this before," Wendy admitted, feeling shy as she brought the sheet up to her chin.

"A chick?" Gabriel asked.

Wendy laughed. "No, taken someone back to my place after just meeting them."

"Oh, well, to be fair, this isn't *your* place so...record still intact."

They both giggled.

"Do you do this a lot?"

"Not *a lot*."

"You're lying," Wendy smirked.

"I'm clean if that's what you're worried about."

"It's not. I've just never been someone's one-night stand before. Not sure what the etiquette is. Do I offer you a beverage? Make you a snack? Pretend to sleep so you can sneak out to avoid an awkward conversation?"

"Like this one?" Gabriel snickered, touching the woman's cheek.

Wendy grinned.

"For the record, this isn't a one-night stand for me. I like you."

"I like you, too."

"Good. So, you ready for round three? Or is it four?"

"Already?"

"I'm insatiable," Gabriel teased.

"Well, I already know *that*," Wendy beamed, scooting closer to kiss her new playmate, running her hand down her body and slipping her fingers once more inside of her. Gabriel pulled her on top of her, holding her face in her hands as she kissed her hard. Wendy's hair fell around her face, enveloping her in a mane of blond, the dim light of the bedside lamp filtering through, lighting up her face in a glowing halo. She was amazing. For the first time in decades, Gabriel was excited to get to know someone. She knew she'd have to leave as soon as she could get a flight, but she didn't want to go. She was happy, an emotion mostly foreign to her. She lost herself in Wendy's warm touch, her soft hair like silk against her skin. Her responsibilities were urgent and many, but for now, they'd just have to wait.

Chapter 6

Lucifer quietly entered Wyatt's apartment, finding Valerie asleep on the living room sofa. "Not very diligent, are we?" he muttered to himself. "Uriel," he whispered, nudging her awake.

"Finally," she complained. "Gabriel won't answer her phone and the vampire's staying away until she's sure he's stopped cutting himself, which he *hasn't*. Every time that boy goes to the bathroom, I end up giving him a lecture about self-harm. I got all the knives and razors out of the house, so this motherfucker broke the mirror and used the shards to slit his wrists again. I can't take it anymore. Can you talk some sense into him?"

"I doubt it. I'm not his favorite person at the moment."

"Then tie his ass to his bed or some shit until he snaps out of it."

"Is that why you called me here? Brute force?"

"You *are* God's strongest or whatever. I'm exhausted and I've missed too much work already. Can you stay with him until Gabriel gets back from wherever the hell she is?"

"I suppose," he agreed, setting his duffel bag on the coffee table. "Where is the poor lamb?"

"Locked in his room," she said, pointing down the hall as she headed for the front door. "Don't kill each other."

Lucifer waited until she'd gone to open his bag and remove a large bottle of whisky. He knocked on the bedroom door and when no answer came, he opened it, breaking the lock with minimal effort. He held the bottle inside, keeping his eyes averted. Wyatt took the offering and slammed the door back. The brothers sat on the floor on either side, Lucifer calm with his hands folded and Wyatt, drinking until his throat hurt.

"I *am* sorry about your son, Barachiel."

Wyatt scoffed. "You would have killed him if I hadn't."

"That's true, and if you weren't so stubborn, I could have spared you from the guilt you're feeling now."

"Go away, Lucifer."

"Afraid I can't. You've given our sister quite the fright and as angry with her as I am for revealing to you the events of that evening, she still deserves peace of mind."

"And what do I deserve?" Wyatt growled. "I'm pretty sure filicide gets you the death penalty in Indiana, except I *can't die*."

Lucifer sighed, wishing there was something he could do to alleviate his brother's suffering. "You only did what had to be done. You always do. It's the burden of what you are. You deserve all the best things this world has to offer, as well as the next. It would serve you well to remember that."

"I deserve to burn."

"You gave that boy a chance, which is more than I would have done. Had he been *my* son, I would have slaughtered him in his crib the moment I learned of his existence."

"That's fucked up."

"Yes, well, God's will and all that."

The two were silent for a while before Wyatt leaned against the door and spoke again, his words slurred. "The only time I don't want to die is when I'm dead."

His pain cut Lucifer like a knife. "It's late. Get some rest, brother. I'll be here."

Chapter 7

"Phindi will have an update for you tomorrow," the young vampire said. "Still no word on Hattie, but I'm happy to serve as your assistant for as long as you need me."

"Thank you, Hart," Allydia replied, slumping in her seat in the throne room, her thoughts with Wyatt. "Tell me, have you ever taken a human lover? Since you became one of us, I mean."

"Not for more than a few days, Your Majesty. They're frail and need constant tending to."

"So you ended things with your human consorts because they were weak?"

"I didn't *break up* with them so much as I *ate* them," he confessed. "In my defense, men these days are *delicious*. Have you ever fed on a fruitarian? *Like candy*."

She smiled. "I have, actually. It's been a while, though."

"Would you like me to send for one?"

"Thank you, Hart. That would be delightful. I could use a little dessert."

"Right away, Your Majesty." He snapped his fingers at the guard standing at the entrance to the room. The man nodded and hurried off. Hart went over his notes before again addressing his Queen. "I've chartered the planes, so that's been handled. All the monthly expenses have been paid. There's just one more order of business."

"What is it?"

He took a deep breath and shifted his weight from one foot to another.

"Hart," she said, her patience wearing thin.

"It's Mason, Your Majesty. He's stirring up trouble. Blaspheming. He's saying…he's telling people…"

"Spit it out, Hart."

"He's saying you're not fit to lead. That you haven't killed in years. That you're soft."

She tilted her head and raised her eyebrows, throwing her hair over her shoulder and clearing her throat.

"Forgive me, my Queen." He looked down at his platform boots and did his best to steady his breathing.

"That's all right." She crossed her legs and sighed dismissively. "More often than not, *someone* has something negative to say. It's not usually worth my time, but, 'not fit to lead'? That's treason."

"Yes, Your Majesty."

"Do you know what my punishment is for treason, Hart?"

"Yes, my Queen."

She twirled her hair and tapped her foot. "I really don't have time for this."

"Would you like me to take care of it, Your Majesty?"

"Only if you can handle it personally. I wouldn't want anyone else thinking I'm too 'soft' to handle my own business."

"Of course."

"Very well. But make sure he understands why he's being punished. Make sure he knows I sent you."

"Yes, Your Majesty."

"All right, you may go. I'd like to be alone with my thoughts."

He bowed and left the room, closing the door behind him.

Allydia's mind wandered again to Wyatt, the blood spilling from his wrist like a siren song. Had he been anyone else, she wouldn't have bothered stifling her baser instincts. As it was, she knew she had to stay away or risk devouring him whole, the image of which she played in her mind like pornography. She would keep a distance, for now, trusting his siblings to keep him safe.

"Hart!" Mason greeted as the Queen's assistant entered the apartment. "I wasn't expecting you. Did we have a date tonight?"

As the door closed, Hart pulled a gun out from under his leather duster and shot the other man in the gut.

"What the hell?!"

"Queen's business."

Mason fell back into a recliner, covering his wound with one shaky hand. "UV bullets?"

Hart nodded.

"You told her? You betrayed me?" His lip quivered under his jet black goatee, blood starting to ooze out from his mouth.

"You know I had to."

"But we are lovers."

He smacked his lips and rolled his eyes. "Getting together a few times a month to bang it out and never speaking otherwise hardly makes us 'lovers'. Besides, my loyalty is to the Queen. You know that."

"Some Queen you serve! Forcing you to do her dirty work, knowing that we were sleeping together. The cruelty!"

"She didn't force anything. I volunteered."

"You...ah. You think you can endear yourself to her."

He clicked his tongue. "She *already* loves me."

Mason wheezed, a knowing smile turning up his lips. "She will never give you what you want."

"You don't know that."

"Foolish boy," he coughed. "She will *never--*"

"Don't call me 'boy'!" His heart beat fast as he shouted.

"You should go home and shave. Your five o'clock shadow is showing."

He pulled his dagger and plunged it into the other vampire's chest. "You shouldn't have blasphemed. You should have kept your trap *shut*."

Mason shook violently as Hart carved, tearing at muscle and breaking through bone. Blood splattered across his face as he reached his hand inside the condemned man's chest.

"Please," Mason gurgled.

He ignored him, got his fingers around the slippery organ, and yanked it from his body. Mason looked at his own heart beating in the man's perfectly manicured hand, the shiny, black nail polish now caked with gore. Hart held it there, showing it to him until the light faded from his eyes.

Death came to all traitors of the Queen, but that wasn't the real punishment. The *real* punishment was watching their hearts beat outside of their body, then stopping. It wasn't enough to kill them. They had to watch, not just feel their lives leave them. They had to be terrified.

It's done, Hart texted. *Is there anything else you need?*

No, the Queen replied. *Thank you. I will see you tomorrow.*

He put his phone on the coffee table and sank into the couch. "Hey, Marilyn," he cooed as his cat climbed up into his lap. He pet her gently as she purred and curled up for a nap. "I missed you, too. Did you have enough to eat while I was gone?" He glanced over to the food dish and saw that there were still a few bits of cat food uneaten. "That's good. Did you have a nice night? Mine kind of sucked. Killed a dude, and not because I was hungry, so that was no fun. Now I have to find a new fuck buddy and you know how I hate shopping for dick. Maybe I'll just be celibate for a while, shut it all down. Put up a sign, 'this booty's closed for repairs'. Not that I'm broken, mind you. Just a little…bent." He tilted his head as he gazed down at his pet as she slept. "You ignoring my existential crisis? That's cool. *I've* been doing it for *years*. The Queen will grant me this, right? She's not *unreasonable*. Just because Mason's like, two hundred or whatever, doesn't mean he knows what he's talking about. Right?"

The cat continued to sleep.

"Fine. You rest. I should probably get some sleep, too. It's been a *night*. Let's go to bed." He carried her to the bedroom and sat her on her princess kitty bed before taking off his boots and letting himself fall into bed, crashing down onto the black comforter and groaning as his face hit the hot pink pillowcase. "So tired."

The cat scratched at the sparkly crown emblem on her bed, licked her paw, and curled up on the plush fabric.

Hart looked over at her one more time and closed his eyes. "Thanks for being a good listener, M."

Chapter 8

Gabriel returned home to Valerie who'd been waiting there, her impatience evident.

"Bitch, where the fuck you been?" she griped. "Me and Lucifer have been taking turns keeping Wyatt from offing himself for *days*. I can't handle this shit."

"I'll go over there after I eat something," Gabriel said, taking a bag of cheese puffs from the pantry.

"Speaking of food, that boy eats *a lot* of pizza. You'd think he was raised by a giant rat in the sewer."

Gabriel laughed. "It's a psychological thing. A 'fuck you' to his dad. He was a very knife-and-fork kind of dude, thought pizza was 'uncivilized', like, peasant food. He was real boujee. Don't tell B that, though. He just thinks he likes it because it's delicious."

"I still can't believe he got back with the vampire. They're a full-blown couple now."

"Right?" Gabriel said, taking a bite and avoiding eye contact.

"Girl."

"Hmm?"

"Girl! You set them up?"

"Only kind of. I didn't *have* to take him to the vampire club to find out where Lilith's demons were. She *could* have told me over the phone."

"The fuck, bitch?"

"I knew she'd get obsessed and start following him around. I knew she'd look out for him, and us in turn, with that whole Lilith thing. I knew she'd protect him. I wasn't counting on him getting so involved, though. I warned him not to get too close. I made it very clear she was--"

"She's a *vampire*," Valerie yelled. "She called *me* because she couldn't handle seeing his blood. What if she--"

"If she ever lays a finger on him, I'll fucking kill her."

Gabriel entered Wyatt's apartment, the stench of booze punching her in the face. Empty pizza boxes lay haphazardly on the coffee table and island while sorrow hung in the air like smog. She looked Wyatt over, his unconscious body on the floor, leaning against the sofa, a nearly empty bottle of scotch in his hand. She took it from him and went to the kitchen where she drained the contents into the sink.

"Gabriel," Lucifer said, looking up from his book. He put it down on the counter and sat up straight on his bar stool. "So good of you to grace us with your presence. Was your trip a success?"

"Not really," she replied, taking the last three bottles of whiskey from the pantry and dumping them, as well. "It's like I thought. He's warded. I did meet a girl, though, so not a total waste of time. What's with the ghost?" She gestured toward the far corner where the phantom that haunted the building stood creepily still, watching in silence.

"The poor dear's been fixated on our bereaved brother. I think she's lonely. Seems harmless enough."

"Ugh, I can't deal with dead people on top of everything else. Yo! Hey, honey! It's time to go home."

"That's rather rude, don't you think?" Lucifer lectured.

"Fine," Gabriel huffed, walking over to speak to the spirit face-to-face. "Hello. I'm Gabriel, Messenger of God. It's time for you to go to Heaven."

The ghost looked at her with hope in her milky eyes before turning her gaze to Wyatt. Worry covered her face as she looked back at Gabriel.

"He'll be fine," Gabriel promised. "I'll stay with him."

The specter didn't look convinced.

"I'm an angel of the highest order. I won't let anything happen to him, I swear. You need to go now. Your baby's waiting for you."

The ghost smiled, looked up, and breathed a sigh of relief as she faded, then disappeared.

"Well, I'm off," Lucifer announced, slipping his book into the duffel bag and zipping it closed. "I could use a decent night's rest. I trust you'll watch over Barachiel, now that you're back."

"As long as he needs me. Listen, you know what's coming. This is gonna be an all-hands-on-deck situation. Uriel can't be fighting with a fucking pocket knife, do you understand what I'm saying?"

"I do, indeed. Have no fear, sister. I know just where to find what she needs."

"Good. And, Lucifer," she said, looking over to Wyatt and back at him. "Thanks."

They exchanged knowing glances as Lucifer picked up his bag. "It was my pleasure." He left the apartment, leaving Gabriel to pick up Wyatt's broken pieces. She took a trash can from the bathroom, set it in her brother's lap, and smacked him in the face. His eyes flew open and she flicked two fingers toward herself, causing the contents of his stomach to come flooding up and out of his mouth. When he was done vomiting, Gabriel took the now full can back to the bathroom before returning and sitting herself down next to Wyatt and patting his knee.

He looked at her, tears filling his eyes as he began to tremble. "I'm not okay," he croaked.

"I know," she told him.

"You were right. About everything."

"See, if you people would just keep that in the back of your minds--"

"How could I do it? What kind of monster am I inside? *I killed my son.*"

"To be fair, he killed you first. I know because I felt that shit. It was brutal. I'm still having nightmares."

"I don't know how to live with this. It's too much."

"I know. Come here." She wrapped her arms around him as he lay his head down in her lap, weeping and grabbing onto his sister's hand, afraid to let go. Tears welled in her eyes, too, as she bent down to kiss the top of his head. She brushed the hair away from his face as she whispered, "I'm sorry. I wish there was something I could've done. God, B, I'm so, so sorry."

"I want to die. I don't want to *exist* without him here."

"Shh." She squeezed him tighter. "I know. The thing is, I need you alive. Valerie's off with her dude most of the time. You're my only friend. Plus, who's gonna put Lucifer in his place if you're gone?"

"I feel like you can handle him on your own."

"Yeah, but Jesus, that's exhausting. He's a handful."

He wiped away another tear.

"I know it sucks. I know how you feel, literally. I'm having a hard time not falling apart, myself. Would it make you feel better if I told you he'll be back someday?"

He sat up. "What do you mean? Isn't he in Heaven?"

"Fuck, no. He killed people. He's in Purgatory. It's like jail for souls. He'll be there for a while, thinking about what he's done, and eventually, he'll be born again. I mean, as someone else, but--"

"When?"

"I don't know."

"How can you *not* know?"

"He's there until he thinks he deserves another chance. He has to forgive himself. Could be a few years, could be a few centuries. It's up to him."

Wyatt stared at his sister, his bloodshot eyes wide and frantic. "Will I see him again?"

"Yeah. I mean, of course. Human souls are never *gone*, just moved. It probably won't be for a long time, though. After Wyatt's dead and you're just Barachiel again."

"Great." He slumped back against the couch and hung his head.

"Sorry. Didn't mean to get your hopes up."

"It's fine."

"He *will* get to Heaven. They all do, eventually. No matter how many times it takes. God doesn't give up on people."

"That's comforting."

"I know you're being sarcastic, but I also know that it *does* make you feel a little better."

He sighed. "Of course you do."

She took out her phone. "I'm ordering food. Not just pizza this time. I'm also getting you some cake."

"Why?"

"You know, sugar, chocolate. It'll make you feel better."

"I don't deserve to feel better."

"Well, I do and I want some cake. Also, that's bullshit. You deserve a medal for what you did for Israel in 1967 alone."

"I have no idea what you're talking about."

"Maybe just trust me then."

He grunted.

"Hey," she tapped his nose with her finger. "Love you."

"Love you, too."

"You'll be all right. Over time."

He nodded but wasn't convinced. They sat in silence, each letting the other grieve in their own way.

Chapter 9

Wendy beamed as she walked to her Chambers Street apartment, lunch from her favorite chicken spot in hand. She couldn't help but smile. It had been a long time since she'd had so much fun with someone. Gabriel was funny, interesting, and to call her 'sexy' would have been a gross understatement. The few days they'd spent together in a Harrisburg hotel room were maybe the best in her life. They'd gotten so lost in all the sex and talking, they'd forgotten to eat. They slept only for a couple of hours at a time; naps between marathon sessions of mind-blowing lovemaking. She'd had more orgasms in the last three days than she'd had probably in her entire life. Just thinking about it got her excitable. The lightness of her touch. The smoothness of her skin. The way she looked up at her with those big brown eyes as she went down--

A chill went through her, her thoughts interrupted by the feeling that someone was following her. She glanced around, seeing no one and quickening her pace. Someone was there. She could feel them closing in, just a few steps behind. She rushed into her building, making a beeline for the empty elevator. As the doors closed behind her, she thought she could finally relax. She was wrong.

"I didn't mean to scare you," the girl claimed as she appeared. "I had to use a cloaking spell so no one would see."

"You're a witch?" Wendy asked, catching her breath.

"They call me 'Poe'. The leather and black lipstick." She gestured to herself and hit the emergency stop button. "You get it. The others don't know I'm here."

"What others?"

"I'm from Grace's coven. She wanted you to have something." The girl, no more than sixteen, held out an envelope. Wendy hesitated before taking it. "Don't open it until you're alone. If the others find out I gave that to you, they'll kill me. Or worse."

"What is it?"

"I can't say." Her eyes darted around the lift. "Not out loud, just in case. You shouldn't, either. They have eyes and ears everywhere." She pulled a newspaper from her jacket and handed it to her. "I marked the page. If you decide to come, use a cloaking spell. If they see you," She shook her head. "Stay hidden."

"How did you find me? I'm shielded."

"Not from your own magic." Poe restarted the elevator. "I was never here, okay?"

Wendy nodded.

The girl was again invisible and as the doors opened to the lobby, Wendy could feel her brush by, leaving her alone. She hit the button for her floor and watched with furrowed brow as the doors again closed. *Her own magic.* That could only mean one thing; Grace must be dead.

She set the bag of chicken on her table and opened the paper to the page with the dog-eared corner. Obituaries. Halfway down the page, she found her great-aunt's name. She'd died of a stroke a few days before. She was ninety-one. Her funeral was set for four o'clock that day.

She opened the take-out container and took a bite of chicken before opening the envelope. Inside was a necklace and note that read, *It's your responsibility now.* She reached inside again and pulled out the cat's eye amulet, a mournful sigh escaping her lips. It burned hot in her hand, radiating power, like the glow from a nuclear reactor. She knew instantly what Grace had done. She'd bound her magic by blood to the amulet, assuring that only a witch that shared her genes would have access to it. It was drawn to her like a magnet, undoubtedly leading Poe right to her.

"Well, I can't deal with *this* right now," she muttered, walking to the desk in the corner of the room and opening the drawer, tossing the necklace inside, and waving a hand over it. "Abscondo." It was now hidden from everyone but her.

She finished eating while contemplating what this all meant. Grace had stayed away, never having made contact with her. Wendy wasn't even sure if her aunt had known she existed. Why would she leave her magic to her? It didn't make sense. Usually, when a witch dies, their power is absorbed by her coven. To bestow her power to anyone outside of the coven would have been seen as a betrayal of the highest order. No wonder Poe had been so afraid. The others must be furious.

Chapter 10

"I'm moving them from Siberia as we speak," Spade told the man on the other end of the call. "I'll join them once I've made arrangements here."

"Will they be ready?" the caller asked.

"Of course. They've been training for years. My soldiers are the best of the best."

"I admire your confidence, Mr. Spade, but you have no idea what you'll be up against."

"We can handle *anything*."

"I hope that's true because your opposition will be unlike any you've ever faced."

"Yes, Lilith told me," he sighed, rolling his eyes. "They have superpowers or something. We have AK-47's. I'm not concerned."

"You weren't privy to all of Lilith's secrets, but trust me when I tell you, she was one of the most powerful creatures to ever walk the Earth and these people took her out in a matter of minutes. Underestimate them at your peril."

"If you say so. I know you don't like me questioning you, sir, but can I ask one thing?"

"If you must."

"The site," Spade wondered. "Why go to all this trouble? Why not just drone-bomb it? Seems so much more efficient."

"It's not enough to destroy the Gate physically, you imbecile. You must also destroy the keepers of it. As long as even one of them remains on Earth, so does the tether."

"You know this sounds like bullshit, right?"

"I would caution you to remember to whom you're speaking."

"I can't remember what I've never been told."

"I'm the man who signs your checks, Mr. Spade. The money Lilith paid plus everything I've been gracious enough to pay you since can all be taken away."

"Yes, sir. I understand."

"Good. Call me with any updates."

As the line went dead and Spade put the phone down, his daughter wandered in, still in her pajamas. "Aubrey!" he called to his wife, who was already rushing to the office.

"I tried to stop her, but she wanted to see you before you left on your business trip," she explained.

"It's all right," he said, his voice calm. "Can you find my passport while I say goodbye to Jenny?"

"Sure," she smiled, leaving father and daughter alone.

"What have you been up to today, Jenny-Bean?" he asked playfully. The girl sat on his knee and giggled. She was eleven with the intellect of a toddler and the communication skills of an infant. She was born with a myriad of mental and physical disabilities, symptoms of her extreme DWS, some of which had been corrected with experimental and impossibly expensive surgeries and treatments. After the influx of money Spade had received by taking the job Lilith had originally offered, he'd been able to pay for all of it, in cash. At nine, Jenny finally took her first steps. Two years later, she was walking almost normally. She still hadn't spoken, but doctors were confident that she could understand when others did. He'd hired a private tutor to teach her to read and write, but she didn't seem to be catching on. It had been a challenge, but Spade was determined to give his daughter the best life he could, no matter the circumstances. "I'll only be gone for a little while," he promised. "A week, I think. Give your mother lots of hugs while I'm away, okay?"

The girl smiled.

"That's my girl," he said, hugging her and kissing her forehead. "That's my good girl."

Chapter 11

Lucifer stood in the center of Saint Michael's Tower on Glastonbury Tor, admiring the craftsmanship of the stonework. It had been centuries since he'd watched it being built, and while it was all that was left of the original building, it was as beautiful as he remembered. All, that is, above ground. As much as he enjoyed a good tourist attraction, he had work to do and he couldn't get to it with all of these people milling around. He looked to the sky through the open roof and allowed a smirk to cross his lips as clouds gathered, thunder sounded and rain poured down. The visitors scattered, covering their heads with picnic blankets and papers, running hastily down the hill. When he was sure everyone was out of harm's way, he walked out onto the grass, hoping his memory was correct about the exact spot. He knelt and placed a hand on the wet ground, causing it to tremble beneath him. As the quake grew in power, the earth opened before him, a wide chasm splitting the clay and shale. He peered down, relieved to see what he'd been after. He stood and jumped in, falling nearly two hundred feet before landing on the stone sarcophagus below. He stepped off and looked it over, noticing how lovely the engravings still were. He tossed the lid off, revealing the ancient skeleton inside, well preserved in the hill's cool conditions. "Hello, Arthur," he said, moving a dragon-embossed banner aside to uncover the corpse's hands, still clutching the Celtic long sword. "Sorry about desecrating your grave, but that's what happens when you're buried with things that don't belong to you." He tore the sword by the horn hilt from the body's grip, almost taking the hand with it. "Do say 'hello' to your sister for me." He winked, leaping up out of the rift. He waved a hand to close the schism as the skies cleared before taking off, flying back to Gabriel's apartment for some much-needed rest, Uriel's sword in hand.

Chapter 12

"It has been a *day*," Valerie griped, plopping herself down on the sofa after a particularly stressful day at work.

"What happened?" Malik asked from the kitchen several feet away.

"Parents whining, mostly. 'Why can't Austin get into Columbia?' 'Why does Xander want to go to film school instead of med school?' It's a lot of 'Why isn't my kid a totally different person than he is' bullshit. *And* I got a visit from the PTA lady, bitching about the safe-sex brochures in my office. Like, sorry, Brenda, but this is high school in Hell's Kitchen, not a fifties sitcom."

Malik chuckled. "Did you say that?"

"No, I put on my fake-polite voice and told her the statistics and how it's the school's policy to prepare kids, blah, blah blah. I still think she left madder than when she came in."

"That place doesn't deserve you."

"Probably not, but the kids need me."

"Speaking of kids, the adoption agency called today."

She sat up straight, her chest tightening. "What'd they say?"

He came out from behind the bar and sat next to her, taking her hand in his. "We got approved."

She covered her mouth as she gasped. "So fast? I thought it'd be--"

"*Approved*, but the waitlist is long. She said it could be up to seven years before we get a baby."

"*Seven years?*"

"I know you're disappointed, but we've been approved. A lot of people don't even make it *that* far."

She nodded and he kissed her hand before heading back to the kitchen, the dinner he was preparing almost ready. He was right. She *was* disappointed, but part of her was relieved. While she desperately longed for a family, a life she could call 'normal', she had always suspected 'normal' wasn't really in the cards for her. Angel business aside, the way she'd grown up had her questioning her abilities as a parent. She had no example of what a good mother looked like. Her grandmother was the closest thing, but by the time she'd met her, she was almost grown and left pretty much to her own devices. If she was being honest with herself, Gabriel had been the most motherly influence in her life. She was always there for her, taking care of her when she needed it, protecting her. She knew her sister worried and cared about her. She loved her. But if *Gabriel* was what Valerie thought a mother was, she was definitely not ready for the responsibility.

"Hey, are you sure--" But before she could finish her sentence, a knock came on the door. "I'll get it," she offered, standing up. "You just keep cooking. Something smells delicious and I'm starving."

"Hello, sister," Lucifer greeted as she opened the door. "How are you this evening? You look tired."

"What do you want? Is Wyatt all right?"

"As far as I know. Gabriel's with him presently. I came to return something to you." He held the sword out to her by its hilt.

"What the fuck?" she muttered, pulling him inside and closing the door, hoping her neighbors didn't see this white boy strolling through the hall with the weapon.

"It's your sword," he explained. "Well, one of them. The only other left on Earth is in an abbey in Tuscany, so in the name of discretion--"

"Why are you bringing me this?"

"There's a battle coming. The world needs Uriel at full power. Pocket knives and kitchen utensils are quaint but relatively useless against an army of paid mercenaries. Speaking of kitchen tools, how are you, Malik?"

Malik grunted from the kitchen as he worked.

Valerie took the sword, the weight of it surprising her. "I don't know how to use this."

"Of course you do, you've just forgotten. Simply do for yourself what you've done for Barachiel. Search your mind for the memories, and do make it snappy. There's not much time."

"Take this to your brother," Malik said, shoving a plastic container into Lucifer's hands. "Chicken, risotto and broccoli rabe. Val told me he's been living on pizza and whiskey. No doubt he could use a home-cooked meal."

"Well, thank you, Malik. That's very thoughtful. I'm sure he'll appreciate the gesture."

"Why is it that even when you're being nice, you sound condescending?"

"It's a mystery."

"Bye, Lucifer," Valerie said, opening the door and pushing him out. She looked over the sword in her hands, a strange sense of nostalgia washing over her.

"Battle?" Malik asked.

"Looks like I need to have a talk with my sister."

Chapter 13

"A gift from Uriel's husband," Lucifer said, setting the container on the counter. "*Uriel's husband.* I don't believe I'll ever get used to that."

Gabriel inspected the contents of the lidded bowl before pushing it away in disgust.

"It's not for you," he reassured her.

"I know, but still."

"How is he?"

"A little better. He's in there taking a shower without breaking anything, so, you know...progress."

"Something's different," Lucifer noticed, glancing around. "Did you clean?"

"Did I *what*? No, I hired a maid service. Did I clean?" she scoffed. "Like I have time for that."

"A sword?" Valerie called as she entered Wyatt's apartment. "Really, bitch?"

"I got you a back-scabbard, too," Gabriel replied. "Lugging that thing around by hand would be--"

"The fuck's goin' on?"

"Keep your voice down," Gabriel ordered. "I don't want to bother B with this until I have to."

"Is he okay?"

"Meh."

"What's happening?"

"Lilith's army is still going after the Gate. I have one more Hail Mary, but if that doesn't work, things are gonna get real bloody. You have to be prepared."

"To fight an *army*? Girl, are you crazy? I'm not a soldier."

"*Valerie's* not, but *Uriel's* one of God's finest. Ask this one," she said, gesturing toward Lucifer. "He can tell you stories."

Lucifer nodded in agreement.

"Fine, but how are the four of *us* supposed to go up against *an army*?"

A sneaky smile crept across Gabriel's face as she took a sip of water before answering, "We'll have backup."

Phindi watched from a distance as her soldiers trained under the night sky. Finding a Krav Maga instructor who was also a vampire had proven impossible, so she'd created one, with her Queen's permission, of course. He was still fairly nervous being around so many of them, but she'd assured him that as long as he did his job, no harm would come to him. Still, training nearly three thousand vampires at once in a field upstate would have been difficult for anyone, let alone a fledgling vampire who hadn't quite gotten the hang of things. He was always hungry and had a hard time controlling his urges, but Phindi kept him and the others in line. As the general in her Queen's army, she had a responsibility to train and protect her subordinates. It was a duty she'd been born for, her father having been a great warrior in the Ndwandwe-Zulu War. She was honored to serve her Queen in such an important role, even if she didn't fully understand who, or what, her soldiers would be fighting against.

Chapter 14

Wendy silently made her way through the natural burial ground, having cloaked herself before entering the cemetery. It had been years since she was last here, or in the quiet town that surrounded it. Not since her grandmother had died. It was as peaceful as ever, the soothing sound of the Pocantico River the only thing she could hear. She loved the city, but the longer she walked, the more she realized how much she'd missed the town, the quiet...the nature.

She trekked through the soft grass, admiring the greenery all around her. The trees whispered in the breeze as she strolled, so at ease in this idyllic location, she'd almost forgotten why she was there. A deer moseyed past, unable to see her thanks to her spell. *Good*, she thought, sure now that the coven, too, would be unaware of her presence.

She made her way through the trees and finally came to the clearing where the funeral was being held. Mourners gathered in a crescent shape a good distance from the altar as one after another shuffled to it, kneeling and whispering their final goodbyes to the body lying there. The shroud wrapped around her great-aunt's corpse was sheer enough that she could just make out the woman's face as she stood over her. Her skin was almost as gray as her hair, her cheeks sunken. But, she looked to be at peace. Wendy smiled, tears forming in her eyes. Grace looked so much like her grandmother and seeing her like this brought back all the pain she'd felt when she'd lost her. She'd hated that she hadn't reconciled with her sister before she died, but she'd understood.

"Why did you do it?" a young woman whispered into the dead witch's ear. Wendy had been so lost in thought, she hadn't noticed her approach. She stepped back but listened intently. "Your magic should have passed to us. Why did you hide it? Without it, we--"

"Julia," another woman warned.

"I'm sorry, but we're all thinking it."

"This *is not* the place."

"I know." She stepped toward the group and stared them down, daring them with her eyes to try to silence her. "But we are flailing. Leaderless. This was Grace's coven and it never occurred to anyone to demand she name a successor."

A few of the witches laughed. "*Demand*? Who would dare demand anything of Grace?" one of them scoffed.

"She would have you shunned for even suggesting someone question her," another said.

"Yes, probably," Julia huffed, throwing her long, red hair over her shoulder. "But she's no longer with us and we are desperate. Without the Tituban magic, we're weak."

"We're *witches*," one of them sneered. "We're anything but weak."

"Compared to what?" she griped. "The other covens? Once they hear of Grace's death, the Dyer's will be coming to pilfer our members and the Gowdies will move to eradicate us completely."

"The other covens fear us," Poe chimed in. Wendy hadn't spotted her until now. She looked small; timid compared to the rest.

"*They feared Grace*," Julia corrected. "Without her power, we are sitting ducks."

"You're paranoid," the first woman told her. "It's been three generations since our coven has been attacked."

"Yes, three generations. Since just after Grace put us together. Others tried to dismantle and destroy us and it was *Grace* that shielded us. It was *Grace* that protected and defended us. It was *Grace* that all other covens feared and respected. Without her and her power, we are nothing."

"Enough," an older witch commanded. "You will not disrespect our founder with your dramatics. We will stand in reverence as she moves on to the Summerlands. We will return her body to the ground and *you will show some respect*."

Julia huffed. "Very well. But we *will* have this discussion."

The group quieted themselves, bowing their heads as another witch knelt before their fallen leader. When everyone had had a turn, a few of them told stories, reminiscing about the many ways Grace had impacted their lives. Healing sick children, delivering justice to men that had wronged them, aiding them financially when they were in need. Wendy was fascinated. She'd never known any of this. Her heart warmed at the knowledge that her great-aunt had lived such a full and happy life, even if without her sister.

Poe stepped forward, addressing the crowd as it was her turn to speak. "As you all know, I was in pretty bad shape when Grace found me. My parents kicked me out. I had nowhere to go. I was living on the streets, sleeping in shelters. One day, I was panhandling, starving, and she told me she knew what I was. I didn't know what she meant at first. She said I could stay with her and she'd teach me. She saved me that day." She wiped away a stray tear, her eye makeup smearing across her cheek. "She showed me how to access and control my magic, do spells. She fed me and bought me clothes. She even left me her house here in town." She choked back her sobs before finishing. "Nothing I could do would ever be enough to repay her for her kindness. I owe her my life."

Another woman wrapped her arm around the girl's shoulders and rubbed her arm. "She'll be greatly missed."

Poe nodded. "I just need a minute." She walked off alone into the woods, unable to stifle the tears that streamed down her face, grief mixed with eyeliner staining her flushed cheeks. Wendy couldn't help but feel sorry for her, the urge to hug her too strong to fight. Poe jumped at her touch. "Who's there?"

"It's me, Wendy," she whispered. "Are you okay?"

Poe looked around wildly. "Shh. If anyone catches you here--"

"I'm leaving. I just wanted to say I'm sorry and I'm glad my aunt had someone that cared about her as much as you. Thanks for being there for her."

Tears again formed in Poe's eyes. She rested her head on Wendy's invisible shoulder, grateful for the comfort. "She was like a mother to me. Way more than my real mom was." She wiped her face with her sleeve and gave Wendy a final squeeze. "All right." She backed away, clearing her throat and pulling herself together. "You have to go."

"I'd tell you to call if you ever need to talk, but--"

"I know. Too dangerous."

"Take care of yourself."

"I always do."

"Bye, Poe."

"Bye."

Before leaving Tarrytown, Wendy stopped at a Thai place for dinner and admired a statue off Old Broadway that had been deemed a landmark. She had missed this place, its history, and lore. It felt old, like stepping back in time. There was a gentleness in the air that swept through her, drawing her in and making her wish she could stay. She promised herself she'd return sometime soon. Maybe, if things worked out with Gabriel, she'd bring her along, show her where she grew up. *Please work out*, she thought as she began the fifty-minute drive back to the city, her thoughts drifting again to the amazing time they'd spent together.

Hours later, she lay awake in bed, her thoughts bouncing between Gabriel and the witches at the funeral. The coven had relied so heavily on Grace's magic. She almost felt guilty for keeping it from them. She knew, though, that it was given to her for a reason. Grace clearly didn't trust her fellow witches with it once she was gone. They didn't seem particularly menacing to Wendy; typical witches, as far as she could tell. Maybe it was as simple as Grace having a change of heart. Maybe she knew, like her grandmother had, that the average witch couldn't handle Tituban magic, and instead of allowing her power to turn her coven into monsters, she chose to bind it, protected by cat's eye, accessible only by shared blood. But had Grace even known there were descendants left? That Wendy existed? She had to. Unless she was so worried about her magic getting into her coven's hands that she'd rather see it locked away forever than risk them using it. Poe had certainly seemed rattled when she had brought the necklace to her. Perhaps they were more dangerous than she knew. "My responsibility."

    She pushed the worry away as memories of Gabriel crept into her mind. She smiled in the dark as she remembered her lips on her skin and her hands on her body. She smelled like chamomile and tasted like strawberries and Wendy couldn't wait to see her again. She ached to feel her on top of her, in her, and around her. She didn't know where things were going with her. If it was just for fun or something that could turn serious. A fling or the beginning of a relationship. They'd exchanged information when they'd gotten back from Pennsylvania. Maybe she'd surprise her for a late-night booty call later. Right now, though, she was too aroused to get out of bed, the visions of Gabriel's body floating in her mind. She slipped her hand underneath the covers and into her pajama bottoms, closing her eyes and taking in a sharp breath. Yes, she'd *definitely* have to stop by Gabriel's place later.

Chapter 15

"So, what's on the agenda?" Lucifer asked as he and Gabriel took their seats on the plane. "Please say unrelenting torture."

"I'm putting a tracker on his phone so I know where he is and I'm hacking his computer to find out exactly how many troops he has and the details of his plan. I know he's still going after the Gate, I just don't know when or how. You're coming with because my powers don't work on him. I need you to keep watch so I can book it if need be."

"Well, this should be painfully boring."

"I hope so, bro. I am not trying to get shot tonight."

"Shot?"

"Yeah, dude. Spade's office is on his pseudo-military base. Base of operations? You know what I mean. We'll be going in when most of the contractors are sleeping, but that place will still be crawling with people, all armed."

Lucifer smiled. "This may be more fun than I thought."

"Don't get excited. This is a recon mission. We can't touch Spade, which means we can't kill him. But, if I know where he's gonna be, I can call in some favors. Get him tied up in so much red tape, he'll maybe decide it's not worth it. Better yet, get him arrested the minute he steps foot in Iraq. So, best behavior. This trip is strictly to get intel. You hear me?"

He groaned.

"Lucifer."

"Fine." He sighed and leaned back in his chair, struggling to get comfortable. "You know, we'd be there by now if you'd let me fly us."

"Stop complaining. It's a private jet. Have some champagne. Take a nap. Enjoy your life."

"Speaking of enjoying life, do you think Barachiel will ever get better, or is his current state of melancholy a permanent affliction?"

"I don't know, man," she confessed. "Dia's with him now, so at least he's not alone. She doesn't really know how to handle stuff like this, though."

"What do you mean?"

"As I was leaving, she saw him sitting on the couch all depressive and shit and I heard her think to herself, 'I just want to fuck him until he's not sad anymore'."

Lucifer chuckled. "You don't know. A distraction might be just the thing he needs. If memory serves, she's quite skilled in that department."

"Oh, shit," Gabriel giggled. "Don't let him hear you say that unless you want him to strangle you again."

"You're still here?" Wyatt grunted as he emerged from his bedroom after a long nap.

Allydia's leather-clad legs hung over the arm of the chair she'd draped herself across. She watched him shuffle to the couch and drop into it, his eyes still barely open. "I will always be here."

"I'm all right. You can go."

"I think we both know neither of those things is true. I would offer you a drink, but your sister warned me against it. Something about a familial predisposition."

"She's probably right, *as always*."

"She cares for you," she told him, detecting the disdain in his tone.

"I know."

"Then why do you sound angry with her?"

"It's not her I'm mad at." He sat up to look her in the eye. "I *hate* this *thing* in me. *I hate him*. 'Protector of Humanity'," he sneered, trembling with rage. "I say, 'him', but he's me. The real me, inside. Lucifer was right. I'll always do what's in the best interest of everyone else, no matter what it costs me. The greater good will *always* come first. That's who I am." Tears welled in his eyes as his voice broke. "What does that mean for me? Should I give up hope of ever being happy? Am I just not built for it? Will I ever have *anything* that's just mine?"

She left the chair and knelt on the floor in front of him, cupping his face in her hands. *"You will have me."*

His features softened as tears spilled onto his cheeks. "I thought I'd pushed you away."

She smiled. "It would take a lot more than an *attitude* to get rid of *me*."

A quiet laugh escaped his lips as he took her hands in his.

"Do you need to talk?"

He shook his head, breathing in her pheromones and letting them work their magic.

"Would you like me to comfort you?" she asked, tugging at his pajama pants.

He nodded, his mind too hazy now to form words.

She smiled again. "Good thing I'm already on my knees."

"Are you nearly finished?" Lucifer complained as Gabriel downloaded the relevant files to a flash drive.

"Just stay there," she ordered.

"This is absurd. We've snuck into the enemy's lair. We should take offensive action *now* to prevent--"

"The people here haven't done anything, yet. We can't just preemptively slaughter thousands of people."

"Of course we can."

"Okay, I'll rephrase. We *shouldn't* slaughter thousands of people. There's a chance they might reconsider. Disobey orders. Bail on the mission."

"They're *soldiers*. It goes against who they are to be defiant."

"I didn't say it was a *good* chance." She started hiding cameras while Lucifer waited outside the door, keeping watch like a burglar too incompetent to be part of the actual crime. He peeked his head in, saw that his sister was thoroughly distracted, and left his post.

He headed to the mess hall, conveniently located at the center of the compound. Directly surrounding that were the barracks where more than one hundred thousand military contractors slept. "It's almost too easy," he smirked. He punched through the walls behind the ovens in the kitchen, tearing out and snapping apart the down gas lines that fed them as he quietly sang 'Devil in Disguise'. He picked up a few forks and threw them in a microwave, setting the timer for five minutes. He smiled to himself as he hurried back to the office, knowing that he'd get a stern talking-to from his sister, but delighting in the forthcoming carnage all the same.

As Lucifer approached the office door, shots rang out and an alarm sounded. He raced inside to find Gabriel on the floor, unconscious and bleeding out, three bullet holes gaping in her chest.

"Spade, I presume," Lucifer seethed, his gaze shifting to the man with the gun.

"Who are you people?" he barked, pointing the revolver at the intruder.

"Did Lilith not tell you? Of course, she didn't. Always with the secrecy, that one. No matter. I'm her brother and this is our sister. Don't worry, she'll be fine in a few minutes."

"What...what have you done with Lilith? I was told she was 'taken out', but--"

"Oh, she's back where she belongs, in a cage, locked away as to prevent her corrupting any more unsuspecting souls. You'll soon be in your own prison of sorts. Tell me, Mitchell, are you a religious man?"

"That's enough," Spade said, shooting Lucifer in the chest.

"Well, that's inconsiderate. Do you treat all of your guests so brutally?"

"How--"

"I'm much stronger than my sister," he explained. "Her body is a part of her, whereas I'm only visiting mine."

Spade fell back, barely catching himself on his desk. Lucifer moved toward him, holding his hand out in front of him. It was repelled by an invisible force; the warding his twin had put in place.

"Pity," he grumbled, gathering Gabriel in his arms. "Ah, well. We'll meet again, very soon, I imagine. I'd tell you to pray for your safety, but, unfortunately for you, God's not on your side in this war." The room shook, a loud explosion booming in the not so far off distance. Lucifer grinned.

"What have you done?" Spade spat.

"Until next time." He took off, flying straight through the ceiling, Gabriel limp as he carried her. He hovered over the base, giddy at the sight of the smoldering buildings. "Sorry, sister," he whispered. "But, you were wrong on this one."

Chapter 16

Eighteen-year-old Gabriel sauntered through the door of her Fairfield home to find Camael there waiting. They'd lived there together for the last few years, both now free from their abusive parents since Cam's had kicked him out, his violent outbursts having frightened them. He ran a hand through his dark, wavy hair as he prepared himself. His bright blue eyes followed his sister as she sat next to him on the sofa. He was *not* looking forward to this conversation. "How is he?"

"He's good," she said. "Calls himself 'Tae'. He's pre-med, runs a travel agency. Smart."

"And he's on board?"

"Took a little convincing. I had to rearrange his furniture with my brain, but," She shrugged.

He chuckled. "At least you didn't have to kill anyone this time."

"That dude had it coming. Uriel was in danger. I was just--"

"I know, I know." He put his hands up in retreat, the smile fading from his unshaven face. "Any luck with Barachiel?"

"No," she said. "It's like he's hidden from me. Every once in a while, I'll get a glimpse. I'll hear a thought or feel him for just a second. I try to break through, asking where he is, but, nothing. It'd be so much easier if I knew his human name. Why didn't God think that was prudent information?"

"Maybe you're not supposed to find him, yet."

"Bro, I *need* to find him *fast*. From the little bit I've seen in his head, he is *fucked up*."

"More than we are?"

She laughed. "Is anyone?"

He smiled and looked down, his demeanor changing. As his thoughts became clear, Gabriel's eyes widened, horror spreading across her face. "*No*," she commanded.

"G,"

"I said, 'no'." She bolted from her seat and ran to the window. "Come on. We have to go before they get here. We can stay with Uriel and her grandmother until we--"

"Uriel doesn't know I exist."

"Well, she *will*. You're not a secret."

"Maybe I should be."

"Stop being dramatic. Get your ass up before I come over there and drag you to the car myself."

"Gabriel, sit down."

"Camael, let's go. *Now*."

"I waited until you found the others. I didn't want you to be alone."

"Cam, please."

"I'm dangerous. I scare my parents. I *killed* yours."

"That was--"

"G, I'm *Wrath*. I serve one purpose. I shouldn't be here."

"But, you *are* here. You know as well as I do, God doesn't make mistakes. You're here for a reason."

"Do you know what that is?"

"Not yet," she admitted, tears forming in her eyes. "I don't know everything all at once. Some things come to me later, when He wants me to know them."

"Well, when the old man fills you in, you know where to find me." He stood, seeing the police car's lights as it pulled into the driveway.

"Cam, no. Please. Please don't leave me."

He held her face in his hands as he tried to make her understand. "It's getting harder to control. I don't want to hurt you." He kissed her forehead before opening the door. "Visit me?"

She nodded as she choked back sobs, covering her mouth as she watched him put his hands up and drop to his knees. She fell to hers as well as he was handcuffed and read his rights. He nodded to her as he was shut inside the car.

You'll be fine, he thought.

'Fine' is a relative term. She nodded back as the car pulled out of the drive. As she cried, she could suddenly

no longer feel the porch beneath her. The colors of the sky and grass muted. *This is a dream*, she realized. She'd had it before, thousands of times over the years. The memory of that day still stung in her mind as one of the worst of her life. She hung there in her past as her body healed, her anger at Cam's confession still haunting her two decades later. Yes, he'd killed her parents, but it wasn't like they hadn't deserved it.

Chapter 17

Lucifer lay Gabriel on the sofa and stood over her, waiting impatiently for her to come to. He folded his arms and began tapping his foot, trying to decide if he should linger or finish the book he'd been reading. He chose the latter, but before he could pick it up from its spot on the ottoman, he was thrown into the television hanging on the wall, shattering the screen. "Murus!" he heard a woman say. He was pinned there, unable to fight his way free.

"That's just impolite," he quipped, seeing the blonde woman emerge from the kitchen.

"What did you do?!" she barked.

"Nothing to *her*, I assure you."

"Obcillo!" His arm snapped at the word, the bones cracking loudly in his ears. He winced but didn't cry out, his pride stronger than any pain. She took her phone from her pocket and began to call nine-one-one, but before she got to the second 'one', Gabriel gasped, her eyes flying open.

"Wendy?" she asked, slowly sitting herself up and placing a hand on her fully healed chest. "Oh, man, that was unpleasant."

"Holy crap," Wendy breathed. "I thought you were dead."

"I was, but just for a few minutes."

She rushed to sit next to Gabriel and examined her shirt, poking a finger through one of the holes. "Are those bullet holes?"

"I'm fine," Gabriel promised.

"Sister," Lucifer called. "You didn't tell me your new friend was a witch."

"Sursum," Wendy spat, dragging him up the wall and pressing him to the ceiling.

Gabriel laughed. "That's hilarious." She kissed her companion and took her hand. "You can let him go. He's my brother."

"He didn't hurt you?"

"He wouldn't dare. He loves me." She looked up at him squirming and giggled. "Don't you, you dumb fuck?"

"Gabriel," he sneered.

"He's all right, I swear."

"If you say so. Occumbo."

And with that, he fell, grunting as he hit the floor. He righted himself and rubbed his arm as it healed.

"What are you doing here?" Gabriel asked.

"The maid let me in," Wendy explained. "I thought we could get breakfast or--" She stopped and looked over at Lucifer whose arm had fully recovered. "Honestly, what the fudge?"

"Well, it seems you have plans," Lucifer chimed. "I'll just be off--"

"You stay where you are," Gabriel commanded through her teeth, holding out her fist, rendering him immobile. He grunted and folded his arms. She turned her attention back to Wendy. "Can we make it lunch? I need to have a chat with my brother."

"Sure," she agreed. "But we need to have a serious talk about what you--"

"I know."

"All right. I'll see you later." She gave her a quick peck before leaving the apartment.

"What the fuck is wrong with you?" she scolded, standing up and dropping her hand, allowing Lucifer to move freely. "Do you have any idea how many people you just murdered?"

"A hundred thousand, give or take."

"It's not funny."

"Perhaps not, but it *was* necessary. Your humanity is clouding your judgment, Gabriel. This is war. We're defending the Gate to Heaven from those that seek to destroy it. As you once said, it's the only reason you and our siblings are here on Earth. *You should remember who you are.*"

"It's maybe *you* that should remember who I am. It's like you forgot that I know things you don't. Those soldiers were regular people. They would have been easy as shit to take down *if* it came to that."

"Yes, but now we don't have to. It's over. Spade's finished."

"He's *what*? Goddamn, you're usually the smart one. Spade will *never* be finished. He's going after the Gate in four days. You took away his army, so now he has to raise a new one."

He scoffed. "He doesn't have time for that."

"He does if he uses what your psychotic twin gave him and, thanks to you, he has no choice. You fucked us."

"I come bearing pasta," Gabriel said, holding the bag of takeout in front of her like a gift.

"I *guess* you can come in," Wendy teased. They sat, opening the containers of cavatappi and bruschetta.

"So, what are you?" Wendy blurted. "Your aura's brighter than anything I've ever seen and it's the color of the freakin' rainbow. That means you have a really strong link to the other side or a powerful spirit guide or--"

"Heaven."

Wendy froze. "Like, Heaven, Heaven? You're kidding, right?"

"I'm a funny bitch, but no."

"So, you're what? A ghost?"

"What? No, girl. I'm Gabriel."

"I know your name."

"*No, I'm Gabriel.*"

"You're...like, from the Bible? The angel? Now I know you're messing with me."

"I'm not."

"Like, told Mary she was gonna have *Jesus*, Gabriel?"

'That's not *exactly* how it went down, but--"

"Are you fucking kidding me?!"

"You're freaking out."

"I am *definitely* freaking out."

"To be fair, you're a witch, so..."

"Witches are human beings."

"I'm *human*. Sort of."

"And your brother? Is he an angel, too?"

"Technically, but he's, um,"

"What?"

"Don't panic."

"Don't panic? You mean *more*?"

"The brother you met was...Lucifer."

"Holy shit!" Wendy gasped, bolting up from her chair.

"It's okay. He won't hurt you."

"He won't? He's *Lucifer*."

"He's not what-- I mean, he *is*, but he's--"

"So, Heaven's real? And Hell? And *God*?"

"Yeah, it's a little different than-- never mind. Listen--"

"God is real?! Am I going to Hell? Should I stop practicing the craft? I try to only use it for good, but--"

"No, He doesn't-- listen, I'll answer all your questions, but two things first. You can't tell anyone about this. Ever."

"Who'd believe me?"

"And, are we okay? I mean, we spent a few awesome days together and I like you, a lot, but this is real new and if you can't handle it, I mean, I'd understand if--"

"I don't know," Wendy admitted. "This is a *lot* of information. I really like you, too, but I'll have to digest this for a while."

"Okay."

They sat in awkward silence for a few moments, eating and taking sips of soda. Wendy put her cup down, folded her arms, and looked Gabriel over. "So, you can have sex?"

She looked up from her lunch. "You know I can." She winked.

She blushed. "I do. I just thought angels, if they even existed, were like perfect, sacred, virginal beings."

Gabriel burst out laughing. "You thought we were *what*? Maybe go back and reread Genesis 6."

"So, the Bible's...accurate?"

"Bits and pieces."

"What other myths are true? Vampires? Demons? Werewolves?"

"Yes, yes, but they're locked up in Hell, so no worries, and yes, it turns out, sometimes."

"Wow."

"Yeah. To be fair, most people think witches are myths, too."

"Yeah, but that took hundreds of years of hiding and propaganda. We *convinced* people not to believe we existed. Religion has--"

"Religion and truth aren't exactly best friends. Most of the time, they're not even casual acquaintances. Perpetuating one generally has nothing to do with the other."

Wendy raised her eyebrows. "I don't know what to do with all this."

"Sit with it. See how you feel after thinking about it for a while, then call me."

Chapter 18

Gabriel let herself into Valerie's apartment and groaned as she plopped herself down on the couch.

"I guess I'll leave you two alone," Malik chuckled, retreating to the bedroom.

"What now?" Valerie sighed, sitting next to her sister.

"Lucifer screwed us with his latest massacre, which I saw coming, but it still pisses me off."

"Massacre?"

"Yeah, but that's not what's bothering me."

"Why the fuck not?"

"I'm worried about Wendy."

"Who the hell's Wendy?"

"My girlfriend, kind of. Maybe. I don't know, man. We just met, but she's goddamn amazing. She's a Tituban witch, super powerful. You remember Violet, Tituba's daughter?"

"No."

"Right. Well, anyway, Wendy's grandma did one of her spells on her. I can't see in her head. I have no idea what she's thinking or feeling, what her life's been like. Being with her is like being on vacation. If she's not talking, it's just *quiet*."

"Well, good. It's about time you find somebody you can deal with for more than a night."

"I may have fucked it up already."

"Course you did."

"She found me a little…dead."

"Girl, what?"

"Long story. Point is, she knows everything. Who I am, what we are. I don't know if she can hang."

"Jesus fuck, bitch. What were you thinkin'?"

"You told Malik," she defended.

"He's my *husband*. We've been together for *years*. And what was I supposed to say when a demon kicked his ass and I set it on fire?"

"The girl found me not breathing with holes in my chest. There was no glossing over that."

"Fine. So, she's not taking it well?"

"Not super well, no. Better than I expected, but,"

"And you like her? For real? Not just for a weekend?"

"I feel like I'm falling for the girl."

"Damn, bitch. I've never heard you talk about somebody like *that*."

"I've only felt like this one other time."

"Really? What happened?"

"My parents killed her."

Valerie's eyes widened. "You wanna unpack that?"

"Nope."

"I guess we're blowing right by it, then. Listen, just give her a little time. A wise woman once told me that it takes a human brain a little time to catch up."

"I know. Anyway, have you made any progress with your sword?"

"You know I haven't."

"Yeah, but I was trying to be nice, you know, nudging you to get your shit together instead of giving you a lecture."

"Appreciated."

"We only have four days, though, so maybe get on it."

"You sure this is something I can do?"

"I'm always sure."

That night, after Gabriel left and Malik had gone to bed, Valerie sat on her living room floor staring at the sword in front of her. "Come on, bitch," she whispered to herself, mustering the courage to relive her memories as Uriel. "We got no time for you to be scared." She took a deep breath and placed one hand on the sword and one on her temple. "Here we go." She closed her eyes and after a few seconds of searching, a flood of images poured into her mind. She saw the sword in her hands, engulfed in flames, mowing down demons after The Fall. She watched as men whose bodies had been all but destroyed by possession fell under her blade, the thick stickiness of their captors peeling away and being sent screaming to cages. She saw herself somewhere in the Middle-East, driving the blade through soldiers of an enemy army. She watched Barachiel follow an old woman to an alley as she fought to protect civilians in Verona. The sound of people wailing as she struck them down, the begging in their eyes, was more than heartbreaking. Her hands, stained with blood, were all she could see. The image stayed with her for several seconds until another finally replaced it. She saw water below her as she hovered above it. Soon, she felt the sweet relief of the sword leaving her hand as she heaved it into Colliford Lake, painfully aware of the wizard watching nearby.

Tears filled her eyes as she opened them, her hands now covering her mouth as she wept. *All those people,* she thought. *I'm a monster*. She got up, leaving the sword where it was, and headed to her room.

"You all right?" Malik wondered, hearing his wife sniffles.

"No," she whimpered, crawling into bed and his arms, resting her head on his chest as she cried. "I'm really not."

Chapter 19

Camael sat alone at a table in the yard, the books from the prison's library the only company he needed most days. As he read, he could feel the stares from the other inmates. They usually kept a safe distance, having seen too many times what happened to men that challenged him. Every once in a while, though, a newbie would decide to pick a fight, thinking if he kicked the ass of the scariest guy here, he'd avoid trouble with anyone else in the future. It never ended well for them.

He shifted his gaze from the pages to the group. They immediately looked away and began nervously talking among themselves. He returned to his book, having no interest in whatever shenanigans they were planning. From the corner of his eye, he could see one of the men standing. He took a shaky step toward him, fists at his sides. "Are you sure that's wise?" Cam asked in his thick Brooklyn accent, not bothering to look up.

The man looked back at the group. They all shook their heads. "It's not worth it," one of them whispered.

"He's right," Cam said, putting his book down and standing up. The other men rushed away, scurrying like rats on a sinking ship, leaving the first man to face him on his own. He mustered his courage and sprang forward. Cam sighed as the man charged. "This is exhausting." With one punch, he knocked his would-be assailant out cold, breaking his cheekbone.

"Oh!" the other men cringed. A guard approached him, contempt flashing in his eyes.

"You saw that, right?" Cam asked. "I tried to warn him. You know I'm trying not to fight no more."

"Yeah, I saw," he said, bending down to revive the prisoner.

"Yo, Lee!" another guard called from the entrance. Cam looked over to meet his gaze. "Visitor."

He followed the guard to the visiting area and was happy to see Gabriel sitting on the other side of the glass, phone already in hand. He sat down and picked up the receiver, smiling from ear to ear. "Every week, like clockwork."

"How are you?" she asked, already knowing the answer.

"I'm all right. How's Barachiel doin'?"

"Still fucked up."

"To be expected, I guess."

She nodded.

"What's with *you*? You look pensive."

"A couple of things. First, Lucifer royally fucked us and now we're gonna have a full-blown war to deal with. I swear to Christ, this motherfucker *never listens*."

He laughed. "Did you expect him to?"

"*No*, but it would be super awesome if he surprised me *just once* by doing what I goddamn tell him to."

"He's a loose cannon, but when the chips are down, you know you can count on him to have your back."

"I'm worried it won't be enough." She pushed her hair behind her ear and let her hand fall, hitting the table with a thud. "I can't get to Spade, Uriel's taking her sweet ass time getting *her* shit together, Barachiel's useless right now, Lucifer's a giant pain in my ass, as usual. This whole thing could go sideways. I could really use your help."

He gestured to his surroundings. "I'm a little tied up."

"It would take nothing to break you out of here."

"We've had this conversation a million times."

She rolled her eyes.

"Remember last time?" he reminded her. "When Lilith was a problem, you begged me to let you get me out of here, and what did I say then?"

She glared daggers at him.

"I said you didn't need me and I was right."

"You never should have confessed."

"I confessed because I'm guilty." They stared at each other for a few moments before he spoke again. "So, what's the other thing you're upset about?"

"It doesn't matter."

"Come on, G. Tell me what's going on."

She let out an annoyed breath. "There's a girl."

"Oh, juicy. Give me the details."

She whispered, "She's a Tituban witch."

He raised his eyebrows.

"*I know*. She tossed Lucifer around like a rag doll. Broke his arm with a *word*. The best thing, though, is I can't hear her thoughts. Her mind is spelled. I can't see in. I can *breathe* around her."

"So, what's the problem?"

"She *kind of* saw me a *little bit* dead. I had to tell her who I was. She freaked out a smidge."

"She'll get over it."

She tilted her head and raised an eyebrow.

"*She's a witch*. If she was normal, maybe you'd have to worry. But someone like *her*, from *that* bloodline...if *anyone* can handle it, it's probably her."

"I hope you're right." Just then, Gabriel's phone buzzed. Her eyes lit up. "It's her."

"Go." He waved her away. "Get outta here."

"Love you."

"Love you, too, sis. Go get your girl."

Chapter 20

Wyatt opened his eyes, the early morning light seeping in through the space between the blackout curtains. He kissed the top of Allydia's head as he carefully moved out from under her to close the drapes, not wanting the sun's rays to hurt her. He knelt next to the bed, studying her sleeping face. He brushed a few stray hairs away from her eyes as he took her in, grateful for her existence in his life. She, more than his siblings, had pulled him back from the brink. He realized as he watched her how much he needed her and how hard it would be to leave her now.

He stood and got dressed before checking the plane ticket on his phone. He sat on the bed and rubbed Allydia's back until she woke. "Hey," he said quietly as she sat up. "I have to go, but I didn't want to leave without--"

"Where?" she asked.

"Back to the house in Southport. I need to pack it up and get it on the market."

"You don't have to do that now. You're grieving."

"I need to get it over with. Putting it off won't make it any easier and thinking about all of his things sitting in an empty house is--"

"Very well," she said, touching his cheek. "I will come with you."

"I appreciate the offer, but I need to do this alone."

"Are you certain?"

He nodded. "I'll be back tomorrow."

"Promise me," she demanded, the worry on her face breaking his heart. "Promise you will return to me."

He took her hand and kissed it. "I promise. I'm not *good*, but I'm done hurting myself."

"I'm worried that you'll abandon me again," she confessed.

"I won't," he swore, tucking her hair behind her ear. "You're what I'm living for, what's keeping me going. You're my survival."

She took his face in her hands and kissed him, the sharpness of his stubble a welcome discomfort. "I'll be here when you get back." He nodded and kissed her cheek before leaving the room, then the apartment. She sat there in the dimness, the sheet pulled up around her, debating whether or not to follow him. She decided against it, not wanting him to feel suffocated by her constant presence. Still, she was concerned, so she picked up her cell and called his sister.

"Hey, Dia," Gabriel answered, sounding half asleep. "Is he okay?"

"Yes, but he's leaving for Southport. He feels it necessary to pack his son's belongings *now*. He wants to be alone, but,"

"On it," Gabriel huffed, ending the call.

Allydia set the phone back on the nightstand and let out a sigh of derision. "That was abrupt."

"Hey," Wendy said, the sound of Gabriel's voice waking her. "What time is it?"

"Early," she whined, throwing her arm around her and closing her eyes. "Go back to sleep."

"Can't. The smell of your chamomile shampoo is getting me hot."

Gabriel laughed. "I'm glad you called."

"Me, too. So, who's calling at," She checked her phone for the time. "Five-thirty in the morning?"

"My brother's girlfriend. He's been in a bad place lately, so she's worried about him. I'll check on him later. He probably needs a little space."

"Lucifer has a girlfriend?"

"Sort of, but I meant my other brother."

"Other? How many of you are there?"

"Millions."

"On Earth?"

"Oh, five."

"I have to admit, I'm still not sure how I feel about this whole thing. Angels, demons, vampires...it's a lot."

"I know. When my sister's husband found out, he *freaked*. It didn't help that a demon attacked him and he had to watch her kill it with a knife she set on fire, but--"

"Um, what?"

"Never mind. Listen, I like you, a lot, but I don't want to push, so if you need some time--"

"I like you, too. It's weird, for sure. If you asked me a week ago if I believed in angels, let alone would have one for a girlfriend, I would have called you crazy, but--"

"Girlfriend?"

"Oh," Wendy said. "Now I'm being the pushy one. Sorry, forget I said anything."

"What if I don't want to forget?"

"Really? You want to jump into something this soon?"

"I mean, I'll give it a shot."

"Awesome." She kissed her softly, breathing her in like oxygen.

"Okay," Gabriel gleaned, sitting up and throwing back the covers. "If I'm up, I should probably--"

"Where do you think you're going?" Wendy, asked, replacing the covers and pulling on Gabriel's arm. "I wasn't kidding about that shampoo. Get your sexy ass back here."

Chapter 21

"What do you mean, ninety percent?!" the man roared.

"I apologize, sir," Spade said. "We were ambushed. I can't explain it. The one calling himself Lilith's brother...I shot him point-blank in the chest and he *didn't flinch.*"

"I told you these creatures would be difficult to kill. How many men do you have left?"

"Not quite ten thousand, sir."

"That won't be enough. You know what you have to do."

"Sir, I can recruit more--"

"There's no time! You have *three days*. Do the spell."

"Sir, with all due respect--"

"Did I stutter?!" the man barked.

"No, sir. I'll do it today."

"*Now*. Our entire way of life is at stake."

"Yes, si--" The call ended, cutting him off and leaving him feeling defeated and annoyed. He stood among the rubble of what used to be the mess hall, cadaver dogs still finding bodies. "You!" he called to the first person he saw, a young contractor who had been the only person in his building to survive the blast.

"Yes, sir," he said, adjusting the sling on his arm as he approached.

"I need a tattoo artist. Make that a hundred. Hell, call every tattoo shop in the state. Get 'em down here now. Tell 'em I'll pay triple. Every soldier left is getting ink."

He paced around the hotel room, his disappointment in Spade clawing at his peace of mind like a jackal. Perhaps he should have chosen another to lead the siege on the Gate. Lilith had been so sure he would be up to the task, but she had been wrong before. He should have known not to trust her judgment. It was too late now, though. They had three days at most to destroy it and while Lilith had wanted it gone to rule over humanity, *his* reasons were more personal.

"Can you please pipe down?" he snapped. "I can't think straight with all of your blubberings."

The young man sniffled, the duct tape over his mouth muffling his cries. He quieted himself as he attempted to break free from his restraints. The chains dug into his wrists as he struggled, pulling ever so slightly away from the radiator and back again. It was useless. The man had him.

"I'm sorry," he said, kneeling in front of him and stroking his cheek. "I shouldn't have raised my voice. Do you forgive me?"

The young man nodded, confusion and fear filling his bloodshot eyes.

"Aaron is your name, isn't it?"

He nodded again.

"You'll have to excuse my curious nature. I couldn't help but check your identification. Your wallet's lovely. Quality craftsmanship. I just love the feeling of real leather, don't you?"

Aaron didn't respond, staring blankly into his captor's inquisitive face.

"I must be going soon. Have you considered my offer?"

Again, he simply stared.

"Will you not answer me, then?" he roared, tearing away the tape from Aaron's lips. He winced and squeezed his eyes shut. "Answer me!"

"I...I don't know what to say."

"Say that you'll join me," the man all but begged. "We can travel the world, dine in the finest restaurants, visit museums, and take in the theater. We can sleep in palaces and watch the sunrise from the Eiffel Tower. You'll want for *nothing*. All you have to do is *stay with me*."

Tears again fell to Aaron's cheeks as he shook his head. "You're crazy."

The man's eyes darkened. He grasped the younger man's face in his hand, unable to stifle the desperation building in his chest. He stood and stormed across the room, flying into a rage. He tore the linens from the bed and threw the pillows. He lifted the television from its spot and smashed it on the floor. "I tried so hard with you! I gave you everything!" He pulled his instrument from its lined steel case and marched back. *"Why won't you love me?!"* He plunged the point deep into Aaron's chest, his eyes bulging as he watched the blood pour from the young man's mouth. The gurgling of his last breath soothed him. He pulled the iron from his body as he calmed himself. He used the comforter to wipe it clean and replaced it in its rightful spot, closing the case and taking a deep breath. "Why don't they ever love me?"

Spade stared at the security feed, watching as the last few soldiers got their marks. He fiddled with the mortar and pestle he'd used to create the special ink for the tattoos; a mixture of graveyard dirt, silver shavings, and his own blood. He felt a twinge of guilt as he sat in his office, knowing that the men and women that served him would never be the same. It had to be done, though. His benefactor had grown impatient and if he had any hope of paying for his daughter's treatments, his mission *had* to succeed. Luckily for him, unlike Lilith, the man had no desire to conquer Iraq or the surrounding countries. He just wanted some ruins blown to shit. But, after seeing what the people that protected it were capable of, he couldn't afford to take risks. He *had* to use Lilith's spell, but before he could trust it in battle, he'd have to test it in the field.

Chapter 22

"Where is she?" Valerie quizzed Lucifer as she entered Gabriel's apartment, sword in hand.

"Nice to see you, too," he said. "She's run off after our bereaved brother who's decided *now* would be an appropriate time to rifle through his dead child's belongings. A bit soon, I think, but I'm no expert on grief, never having felt it myself."

"When she gets back, tell her I'm *out*," she stated, placing the sword on the island. "I got a glimpse of the horrific shit I did back in the day and I want *no part* of whatever it is you two got goin' on. *I'm done.*"

"Horrific? Don't be so melodramatic, Uriel."

"My name is 'Valerie'. Uriel is a sociopath with a habit of slaughtering folks."

"Come now, sister," he guffawed, rolling his eyes. "The people you killed in the past all had it coming, I can assure you."

"It doesn't matter. I'm not a murderer. I won't--" Just then, a thud came on the door. As Lucifer began to walk toward it, the door crashed down into the apartment. A man wearing a sling stepped inside. His face was still and emotionless, his eyes appearing dead.

"And who might you be?" Lucifer asked. The man didn't speak. Instead, he rushed toward them, using his good arm to knock Lucifer back before turning his attention to Valerie. As he came for her, she acted on pure instinct, grasping the hilt of her sword, swinging it back, and cleanly lopping off the head of the intruder.

"I'm a fuckin' monster," She dropped her blade, hands trembling as the weapon hit the floor and the man's body fell.

"You're not," Lucifer told her, kneeling and looking inside the decapitated head's mouth. "You're an agent of the Almighty, doing what He set you upon the Earth to do. This, on the other hand," He pulled down the bottom lip and showed her the word printed on the inside. "*This is a monster.*"

Chapter 23

You were right, Lucifer thought to Gabriel. *One of Spade's creatures attacked. Uriel handled it nicely. I'm confident she'll be ready when the time comes to go to battle.*

For real, I need you to stop questioning me, she warned as she walked up the steps to the porch. *I do actually know what I'm doing.*

Fine, fine. Have you convinced Barachiel to join our efforts, or is he still too wretched to be of use?

Working on it. She stood at the door for a while, listening to Wyatt inside. He'd packed up most of the house and was sitting on the couch, holding one of Will's tee shirts and weeping. She noticed the pile of boxes on the porch and the open moving van in the drive. To kill some time while she gave her brother a moment, she began loading boxes. Halfway to the truck, she set the first box on the sidewalk. "Seems inefficient." She looked around at the empty street and vacant fields surrounding the property. When she was sure no one was there to see, she waved her hand at one box after another, loading them onto the truck telekinetically.

"What are you doing here?" Wyatt asked from the doorway.

"Helping you move? That's what family's for, right?"

"I don't need a babysitter," he told her. "Anymore."

She walked towards him to get a better sense of what he was feeling. He wasn't lying. The suicidal thoughts were gone and while he was still crushed, he was relatively functional. "Yeah, well, maybe I needed to say 'goodbye', too."

He nodded and stepped aside, letting her walk into the house. She glanced around the living room, nostalgia sweeping through her. The air was different here. Still. She'd only been there a dozen or so times, but it was strangely comforting, somehow feeling like home. Or, maybe it was her brother's presence. His mental state had settled a bit and she was no longer brought to tears just by being near him. She could feel the tears coming, though, her own grief threatening to bubble to the surface any minute.

"Remember when he made me give him a horsey ride right there?" she reminisced, pointing to the floor near the entrance to the kitchen. "*Twenty minutes*. My back hurts just thinking about it."

Wyatt laughed.

"The first time he told me he loved me, he must have been around three, he grabbed my face and kissed my cheek and said, 'I love you, Aunt Gabriel'." She wiped a tear away as she spoke. "It was the first time someone had ever said that to me where I didn't feel like they felt obligated to. I'm not an emotional person, usually, but goddamn it, I loved that kid."

Wyatt pulled his sister in for a hug and kissed the top of her head as she cried, tears welling in his eyes, as well. She sobbed into his chest, allowing herself, finally, to feel the loss wholly. She'd been avoiding it, keeping herself distracted. She had to be strong for the others, to make sure they stayed focused, but Wyatt was different. She knew he would do as she asked simply because it was the right thing to do. He didn't need to be scolded or threatened or harped at. She could relax when it was just the two of them and at that moment, she could not have been more grateful to have found him.

"All right," she said, pulling herself together. "What is there to eat around here?"

"There's still a lasagna in the freezer," he shrugged.

"Well, heat that bitch up. I'm starving."

They sat quietly, eating straight from the pan, the plates already packed and on the truck. "It's nice out here," she observed. "Peaceful."

"Yeah," Wyatt agreed. "And boring, and lonely."

"Still, it's good to have a place far away from people. The only thoughts I can hear are yours. No neighbors stressed out about the news or health issues. No one worried about relatives overseas or wondering if their high school crush likes them back. It's soothing."

"I suppose."

"Let me buy it."

"The house?"

"Yeah. You're selling it, anyway. I could use a place to get away from everything, especially once this whole golem thing is over."

"The what?"

"The other reason I came by," she said, putting her fork down and taking a sip of soda. "Long story short, Lilith's army is still going after the Gate. We have a few days to get our shit together and haul ass to old Babylon to protect it. It was already a nightmare, then Lucifer decided to go rogue and kill off most of the soldiers, so Lilith's general, a guy named Mitchell Spade, you know, the Cardinal Rain guy? He used a spell Lilith left for him, like a break-glass-in-case-of-emergency sort of thing, and turned what's left of his army into golem. Basically, puppets that'll do anything he wants. They can't be hurt by anything living. Luckily for us, your girl is providing *her* army of undeads to kill them all while I hold them back from the Gate and Lucifer takes out tanks and drones. Still not sure how to stop Spade, himself, though. Lilith warded him. Anyway, your lightning skills would come in real handy, but I'd totally understand if you're not up to it."

He glared at her. "You just said a lot of things."

She shrugged and nodded in agreement.

He leaned back in his chair and folded his arms. "When do you need an answer?"

She looked at her phone, reading the text from the pilot saying the jet was gassed up and ready for departure. "I have to go," she said, getting up from the table. "You have an eleven-hour drive to think about it."

Chapter 24

"I just don't know what to do now," Ms. Landry sniffed, sitting down across from Valerie, the desk between them more cluttered than usual. "The after-school drama program is *working*. Giving these kids an outlet, keeping them out of trouble. They'll be devastated."

"Man, these budget cuts are out of control," Valerie bemoaned. "Did you know they're getting rid of SAT prep? They say their goal is to get every kid 'college-ready'. How do they expect--"

"Ms. Moore," the principal's secretary said, poking her head into the office.

"Hey, Karen."

"Principal Simpson would like to see you."

"Oh, lord," she said, getting up and heading to the door.

"Good luck," Ms. Landry said, patting her arm as she walked by.

"Thanks, girl. I'm probably gonna need it." As she walked across the hall to the principal's office, she was almost run over by the boys' gym teacher. His face was red and he muttered obscenities under his breath as he passed. "That's not encouraging," she uttered to herself as she went in.

"Ms. Moore, have a seat," the weary principal offered.

"What's going on? Andrea's in my office on the verge of tears and Bill just came out of here lookin' like you smacked his momma."

"It's the damn budget cuts," he grumbled. "I'm having to make some tough and, admittedly, unfortunate decisions."

"It's really that bad?"

"It's worse. I hate to do this, but I have no choice. I have to knock you down to part-time. Two days a week, a third of your current salary."

"The fu--" She stopped herself. "Sorry, I mean, what?!"

"I know," He rubbed his temples. "I know. But my hands are tied. Even with all the cuts, we'll barely have enough money to keep the lights on. Mentoring programs, after-school programs, all gone. Any teacher without tenure will be replaced by a newbie at half the salary. The union's gonna have a field day with that one. I really am sorry. I wish there was something I could do."

"All right, you know what? There is no way I'm trying to do this shit *part-time*. I'm a guidance counselor, not a cashier. If I wanted to work for less money than it takes to live, I wouldn't have worked my ass off putting myself through college. I tried to be professional, but *fuck this*. I quit."

"Ms. Moore, please don't--"

"It's Mrs. Perry and I've got more important things to do, anyway."

Chapter 25

"Fair warning, Uriel's in a mood," Lucifer said as Gabriel entered the apartment. "She's on the roof, honing her swashbuckling skills. I offered to assist, but she said if I dare follow her, she'd lop my head off the way she did the golem this morning."

"Fucking Lilith," she complained. "Ten thousand golem we have to deal with now. Next time I tell you not to kill people, can you just listen? For fuck's sake. No, you know what? After we secure the Gate, maybe just don't kill anyone ever. How 'bout that?"

"You really know how to take all the fun out of being alive, don't you?"

She rolled her eyes.

"Perhaps if you'd be willing to share more vital information, we wouldn't be in this predicament."

"You know I can't."

"Yes, yes. God's 'need-to-know' policy. You know all and the rest of us are left scrambling."

"I don't know *all*," she asserted. "Just more than *you*, so it would be super helpful if you could just trust me."

"It's not that I don't trust you, it's that I'm impatient and impulsive."

"Maybe something to work on."

"Speaking of things that would be helpful," he cajoled. "Now that our enemies are no longer human, your witch friend could prove useful."

"No."

"Think about it, sister. A Tituban witch *happens* to fall in your lap just as we're in need of--"

"I said 'no'."

"You're being unreasonable."

"Probably."

"Gabriel,"

"I'm not putting her in danger."

"She's a *Tituban witch*. She's hardly defenseless."

"She's still human."

"What do you remember of Salem?"

"It doesn't--"

"Children attempting to summon me, demons torturing them instead. Tituba was the only real witch among them. *She* drove out the demons on her own. I didn't have to lift a finger. No other witch in history had that kind of power. None human, anyway."

"Wendy isn't Tituba. She's a white girl from Tribeca. The genes are so watered down--"

"Perhaps, but if she possesses a tenth of her ancestor's power, she's still the strongest enchantress on Earth. Do you honestly think meeting her now was a coincidence?"

"No," she conceded.

"Then find out what she's capable of. You're derelict in your duty to our Father if you don't use every weapon available to contain this threat."

"Trying to give me dad-guilt?"

"Never. Just trying to win this war."

Valerie was getting used to the weight of the sword as she grew more comfortable with every swing. The setting sun's light glinted off the steel as she sliced through the air, again and again, her anger fueling her effort. Furious and resentful, she threw the blade, embedding it in the building, barely missing her sister's face as she stepped onto the roof.

"I should have brought you some fries to go with all that salt," Gabriel teased.

"Unfunny," she huffed as she pulled the sword from the stone.

"Sorry about your job. I know it meant a lot to you."

"Gives me more time to kill monsters, right?"

"I know it's not what you want to be doing, but--"

"I know, I know. God's will or whatever. Is this it, though? This fight with the monster army? Is our angel-work done after this?"

"Well,"

"Man, what the fuck?! How long is this gonna go on?"

"Just like, three or so years, give or take."

"So you're telling me I have to tell my husband we can't have a baby for at least three years? If the adoption agency calls, I have to tell them 'not right now'?"

"I didn't say that."

"Well, bitch, I'm not trying to raise a kid in the middle of this bullshit! Everywhere I go, something's trying to kill me."

"I mean, I see what you're saying, but--"

"So, what's up with your girl? Lucifer thinks--"

"I know what Lucifer thinks."

"Well? If she's as powerful as he says she is, maybe--"

"She could get hurt."

"Girl, so could we. Besides, you're the one that keeps telling me our mission is the most important thing in the world. That still true?"

She folded her arms. "Yes, and Lucifer's *probably* right. Don't tell him I said that. If his head gets any bigger, his neck won't be able to support it."

Valerie laughed. "What about Wyatt? Is he coming, or is he still too fucked up?"

"He's thinking about it."

Wyatt ate in the cab of the moving van, not feeling up to being around strangers. He'd driven in silence, mulling over everything Gabriel had told him. He needed more information. He sat his sandwich on its wrapper and called Allydia. The sun had been down for hours; she should be awake.

"Yes, darling?" she answered.

"Hey, what can you tell me about golem?"

"You spoke to your sister. I hope you're not angry with me for keeping you in the dark. I didn't want to burden you."

"No, I understand."

"Thank you. So, golem are living dolls, bound to their creator by blood magic. They're fiercely loyal and will carry out his wishes even without him having to say a word. They feel nothing. They're creatures of blind obedience."

"Do you need me?"

"I always need you."

He smiled for a moment. "For the fight."

"Oh, I don't know. My soldiers are quite capable. Still, the last time I talked to your sister, her heart was beating more rapidly than usual. I'd dare say she was nervous."

"If *she's* nervous, it must be pretty bad."

"Yes, I suppose it is."

"All right. I'll be home in a few hours."

"I'll see you soon, then."

He ended the call and went back to his sandwich, thinking as he chewed. He was tired, not physically or mentally fit for battle, but what choice did he have? It was the *Gate to Heaven*. He knew how important protecting it was, that it was the reason he and his siblings were born. It was why Lucifer was on Earth. It was why he'd had to put that poor girl that Lilith had been possessing in a coma. While an army of golem was the *last* thing he wanted to deal with, his family needed him; the only family he had left.

He bagged up his trash and took it to the bin next to the entrance. He noticed, through the glass door, the many people sitting down together, enjoying their meals. Couples and families, laughing and talking, oblivious to the dangers Gabriel wanted him to help her fight against. He knew it was big. Even Allydia was offering up her army to aid in the battle. As he watched a young boy dip a french fry into a shake, a tear came to his eye. He couldn't let anything bad happen to anyone else's son. He got back in the truck and began the last two hours of his trip home. As he pulled onto the highway, he thought to his sister, *Looks like we're saving the world.*

Chapter 26

A guard Camael had never seen before opened the cell door, waking him from a dreamless sleep. "Move it, Lee." He shot the guard a confused glare but followed him to the visiting area. He was surprised to see Gabriel there, impatiently waving him over.

He sat in front of her and picked up the phone. "It's the middle of the night. How'd you arrange this?"

"I'm rich."

"Oh, right," he laughed. "So, twice in one week. What's the occasion?"

"I need your counsel."

He raised an eyebrow in interest.

"Lucifer and Uriel think I should ask Wendy to help with the Gate."

"You probably should."

"Damn it, Cam. You, too?"

"You came for my opinion, right?"

She grunted, then nodded.

"She's a witch. She could help."

"Something could happen to her."

"Again, *she's a witch*. You probably don't need to worry about her so much."

"I worry about *everyone* I care about."

He tilted his head and smiled, his eyes wide.

"I think I'm falling for her. I mean, hard to say, but it's like...it's kind of like--"

"Ada?"

Gabriel's face fell. "Not exactly. Wendy and I don't have to *hide*."

His features softened. "You never had to hide from *me*."

"I know, and I appreciate you, more than you know. This girl, though. Dude, I'm *concerned*."

"I think she'll be fine. What's the worst that can happen? If she gets hurt, you can just heal her."

"It's not only that. What if she sees it, what it's actually like to be with me? The monsters and the killing. What if she decides it's too much?"

"Some unsolicited advice?"

"Why not?"

"It sounds to me like you love her. As far as I know, that's only happened for you one other time, so if there's a chick out there giving you the warm and fuzzies, I say enjoy it. You deserve to be happy, despite what you think about yourself most of the time."

"What if she bolts?"

"Then you'll be sad for a while. Who cares? Wouldn't you rather have something amazing for a little while than sentence yourself to a life in solitary?"

"I see what you did there."

"Don't worry so much about it ending that you push her away."

"That's some strong wisdom, bro."

"I'm in prison. All I have to do all day is work out and read."

They both laughed.

"Listen, get through the next couple days, defend our way home, defeat the bad guys, and then have some fun. Take your girl on a trip. Somewhere tropical. A beach. Chicks love beaches."

She bit her bottom lip and chuckled.

"I mean it. Get out of town for a while. Go on vacation."

"I can't leave. Barachiel--"

"Is a grown man, with the Queen of all vampires lookin' out for him. What are you worried about? It's not like he can die. I know you feel guilty about what happened when we were kids, but you can't beat yourself up over that forever. At some point, you have to forgive yourself and live your life."

"I'll consider it. All right, I'm gonna go talk to Wendy. Maybe she can give me a charm or something to break Lilith's warding. I'll see you next week. Love you."

"Love you, too." He waited until she disappeared behind the door before standing to go back to his cell.

"*Goddamn*, your sister is *hot as shit*," the guard blurted.

"What did you just say to me?"

"She slipped me a grand to sneak her in tonight, but with tits like that, I would have done it for a lot less, if you know what I'm sayin'. Tell her next time she can visit whenever she wants, *if* she spends some time with *me*, that is."

Camael gripped the guard by the throat and threw him into the wall. "The fuck did you say?!" He grabbed the back of his head and slammed it onto the table. "That wasn't very polite." He gritted his teeth, his whole body shaking with rage. He took the phone from its cradle and smashed it into the man's temple, again and again, sending blood and bits of flesh flying. His skull shattered, the impact of Cam's blows growing in strength as he relented to his impulses. When the guard's head was little more than a puddle, he dropped the phone and backed away, his chest heaving as he struggled to calm himself. He looked at his reflection in the glass, the blood splattered on his face and clothes filling him with shame. His shoulders slumped and he looked down at the floor. "I'm sorry." He took the keys from the guard's belt and turned to take the long walk back to his cell. Once there, he locked himself back in and hid the keys in a hole he'd dug into the wall, carefully placing the poster back over it. He washed away the blood as best he could, assuming the guard had turned off the security cameras before retrieving him. The block was quiet. If anyone had been awake to see him, they weren't saying a word. And they wouldn't. They wouldn't dare risk that he'd come after them next. This wasn't the first time Cam had lost his temper, and every prisoner there knew what he was capable of. Unfortunately for the rookie guard, no one had given him the memo.

Chapter 27

Gabriel took Wendy's face in her hands and kissed her hard.

"Well, hello," Wendy giggled, closing the door as Gabriel entered the apartment. "It's late. Everything all right?"

"I have to ask you something," Gabriel hesitated. "I don't want to. I wanted to keep you as far away from this as possible, but you might be our only hope."

"Your only hope for what?"

She cringed a little before saying it. "Saving the world."

She laughed.

"I'm not kidding."

"What are you talking about?"

"There's a place in what used to be Babylon. We, my siblings and I, have to protect it, like, at *all costs* and there's an army of golem headed there *right now* on a mission to destroy it. You're a witch, so--"

"Hold on. You and your siblings, the *angels*, are in a war with *golem*? The clay to life puppet monsters from Jewish folklore?"

"Sort of. Religion never really gets the details right. Doesn't matter. Point is, if they blow this place up, me and my family don't get to go home when we die. *No one* gets to go to Heaven when they die. My Father's plans get flushed down the toilet and we're all pretty much fucked for the next two hundred and forty years."

"Your Father...you mean *God.*"

"Yeah."

Wendy's eyes were wide, eyebrows raised. She didn't hesitate. "Tell me what you need. It's yours."

"A protection spell. Something to guard the place while we take out the baddies. Maybe something to remove warding? Give me whatever ingredients and words to say and I'll--"

"That's not how it works. Something that powerful I'd have to do myself. No offense to you, but you're no witch. Even if you were, my spells are too strong for most to handle."

"Okay. Never mind, then. I'll figure something else out. I always do."

"Don't be crazy. I'm coming with you."

"No."

"Gabriel,"

"I won't put you in danger. If something happened to you--"

"I can take care of myself. Not to toot my own horn, but I'm pretty badass. Besides, it's for *God*. Who am I to say no?"

Tears formed in Gabriel's eyes as she feebly tried to wave them away.

"Why are you crying?" Wendy asked, touching her girlfriend's hair and cheek.

"I don't want you to get hurt."

She kissed her and wiped away her tears. "It's sweet of you to worry about me, but you don't have to."

"You'll see things...see me do things. I'm afraid you'll think less of me. Be afraid of me."

Wendy laughed. "I'm not exactly a stranger to spooky shit."

"Aren't you scared?"

"Of course, it's an army of monsters with guns. I'm badass, not stupid."

"I didn't mean about the war."

Wendy looked at her fondly. "A little. But, you're pretty cute, so I think I'll risk it." They both laughed before kissing again. "So, when do we leave?"

Chapter 28

"Three years?" Malik asked.

"That's what she tells me," Valerie huffed.

"And she swore it'd all be over then? No more fights with this demon or that mythical creature? You'd be free?"

"Supposedly."

"Well, okay. That's not that long. Hell, we'll probably still be on the waitlist. Plus, it gives us time to find the perfect house, settle in, get a minivan."

"A minivan? Who are you right now?"

He laughed. "I'm just excited to start our family. Maybe not a minivan. An SUV?"

"We'll talk about it." Her face fell, her expression solemn.

"What's wrong?"

"What if I'm not cut out for it? Parenting, I mean."

"What are you talking about?"

"You know, growing up in foster care, bouncing around, all the abusive shit. I don't know how to be a mother."

"Val, up until this morning, you were a *guidance counselor*. *Your job* was helping kids."

"High school kids, picking colleges, classes, and careers. Their parents did all the actual work. I just helped them get to where they wanted to be."

"Well, Val," he chortled. "What do you think parenting is?"

"That's the problem. I couldn't tell you."

"Baby, all it is is giving them what they need to become the people they want to be...and keeping them alive." He winked.

"Oh, shit. I didn't think about it before now, but how's it gonna be for them, having *Lucifer* for an uncle?"

They both laughed.

"Well, I don't know. Maybe he only visits when your sister's around. She seems to keep him on a pretty tight leash most of the time."

"She *tries*." She covered her mouth as she giggled.

He took her hand. "You have nothing to worry about. I'm a thousand percent sure you're gonna be an excellent mother."

"How?"

"Because I know you, better than anyone."

"Do you?"

"Well, maybe not as well as your sister. She has the advantage of being able to read your mind." He smiled. "Speaking of, wouldn't she try to talk you out of it if she thought you weren't mother material?"

"Yeah, she's not shy about telling me what she thinks I should or shouldn't do."

"No. So can you stop second-guessing yourself now? Unless there's something else goin' on."

"What do you mean?"

"I mean, if you don't *want* kids--"

"Oh, no, I do. I definitely do. I'm just afraid I'm gonna mess them up."

He kissed her hand. "Every parent worries about that. *Especially* the good ones."

"I guess."

"So, tell me about this thing you're getting ready to do. How dangerous is it?"

"Extremely. I'll basically be beheading dudes in the desert for as long as it takes Lucifer to disable bombs. An army of vamps will be doing most of the fighting, I think, but it'll be a miracle if I don't get shot."

"And I'm supposed to be okay with this?"

She shrugged. "Not really. Shit, *I'm* not okay with it, but if Wyatt can drag his ass out there after everything he's been through lately, I have got no excuse to sit mine at home."

Chapter 29

Wyatt walked into his apartment after leaving the contents of the moving truck in a storage unit on West 55th. It was late and he felt drained. He kicked off his shoes and collapsed onto the sofa, barely able to keep his eyes open.

"Mr. Sinclair," a voice called from behind.

He sat up, turning his head to see a man he didn't recognize sipping from a blood bag.

"I'm Hart, the Queen's assistant. She wants me to tell you she's attending to her army, but she'll be back in a flash." He came around to the front of the couch and looked Wyatt up and down, taking another sip and nodding in approval. "Okay, I get it now."

"She could have left a note."

"She wanted me to make sure you were all right. You need anything? I can order you some take-out, give you a massage, run you a bath. *Anything* you want."

"I'm fine."

"I can see that."

"I thought that girl, Hattie, was her assistant."

"Mmm," Hart acknowledged, sitting next to him and rolling his eyes. "She *was*, but she disappeared without a trace a couple of weeks ago. Rumor has it, she sired a new vampire without the Queen's approval. I don't know if that's true, but if it is, best she stays away *for good*."

"Why's that?"

Hart put his hand to his chest. "Are you kidding? Have you ever seen Her Majesty angry? I wouldn't wish her wrath on my worst enemy."

"Really? She seems so,"

"Fair? Generous? Kind? Loving, even?"

Wyatt nodded.

"She is. But, get on her bad side," he shook his head. "I don't recommend it."

"Good to know," he chuckled. "I appreciate that she cares enough to send you, but I'm all right. I'm just gonna go to bed. You can leave."

"I can't. As rude as it is for me to stay when you want me to go, if I leave before the Queen gets back, she'll skin me alive."

"You mean that metaphorically, right?"

Hart took another sip from his blood bag, his eyes fixed on Wyatt's, and shook his head.

Chapter 30

Allydia looked over her soldiers, arms folded and a scowl on her face. Red war paint had been smeared in stripes on their cheeks to symbolize the blood-bond they all shared. Some carried swords, others machetes. Some held no weapons, instead relying on their hands to do the work of removing head from body. Those were the ones that gave her the most pride...and the most concern.

"Are they ready?"

"Yes, my Queen," Phindi said confidently. "They have been trained in the ways of the Israeli's, as you commanded. I would trust any one of them with my life, in battle or otherwise."

"Thank you, Commander. You've proven yourself invaluable. Should we prevail, I will give to you anything you desire. Money, title. Simply name it and it's yours."

"You are very kind, Your Majesty. But, you have already been so generous. I require nothing but to keep serving you as long as I am needed."

"It's not about what you *require*. It's about what you *deserve*. Come out of this with your head and heart intact and I will give you the world on a platter."

Phindi stood straight, honored, and proud. "Whatever you wish, my Queen."

"It's nearly morning. Get some rest. When the sun sets again, make sure everyone's well fed. They'll need their strength."

She nodded. "The plane's windows have been blacked out. We will sleep there so there will be no delay in our departure." She turned to face the soldiers and gave the order. "Planes, now!" The soldiers spun on their heels and began to file into the five double-deck aircraft Hart had chartered.

"I will meet you there. Remember, keep everyone on the planes until I arrive. I don't have to tell you how unforgiving the desert sun is to things like us."

"Yes, my Queen." She bowed and made her way to the lead plane, leaving Allydia alone on the tarmac. She sighed heavily. She hated putting her people in harm's way. But the fight was just and besides, this was the last favor she owed. After this battle, it would be Gabriel's turn to deliver on her part of their arrangement.

"He's all right, I trust," Allydia said as she entered the apartment, closing the door behind her and taking a seat at the kitchen island.

"Yes, Your Majesty," Hart assured her, hurrying to fetch her a blood bag from the fridge and tossing it the microwave. "He's been asleep for just over two hours."

"Good. Thank you, Hart. The sun will be up soon. You may go."

"Actually, there's something I'd like to discuss with you, if I may." He removed the blood from the appliance and poured it into a glass before handing it to her and kneeling, his eyes fixed firmly on the floor.

"Of course. What is it?"

"I've been struggling with how to bring this up, and I know it's maybe not the ideal time, a war on and everything, but--"

"You have a request?"

"I do," he told her, his voice shaky.

"All you need to do is ask."

"Okay," he gulped. "Your Majesty, I want to...I *need* to..."

"Yes?"

"I'd like to...transition."

She burst into laughter, setting her glass on the counter. "Hart, remind me of the night you turned."

He shifted a little as he remembered. "It was the summer of 1969. I was outside a club in Greenwich. Some guys had beaten me up. I was bleeding from the head. I tried calling out for help, but it was so crazy, I didn't think anyone heard me. But then, you came. You asked if I wanted to live a life free of hate and fear."

"And have I provided you with that life?"

"Yes, Your Majesty."

Her voice softened. "Then why would you think you had to ask my permission to be who you are?"

Tears started to form in his eyes.

"Look at me," she ordered. He raised his eyes to meet hers, the tears now spilling out. "I don't care what you look like or what you identify as. Change your clothes, change your name, change your gender. It's all just window dressing to me." She touched his cheek and smiled. "You're perfect. You've always been perfect. And, whoever you become, however you wish to present yourself to the world, you will always be perfect to me."

Hart covered his mouth, muffling the sobs he didn't want her to hear. He did his best to gather himself before standing. "Thank you, Your Majesty." He hurried to the door, locking it behind him as he left.

Allydia went to Wyatt's bedroom where she found him standing in the doorway, having listened in on her conversation. He took her face in his hands and kissed her sweetly. "You don't seem scary to me."

"I don't? Maybe you don't know me as well as you think you do."

He laughed. "You're probably right about that."

Chapter 31

Hart woke early the next night, having set an alarm for just after sunset. He was too excited to start his new life to sleep in. He tied back his shoulder-length hair and slipped on a satin robe before heading to the bathroom. In a rush, he applied the shaving cream and lifted the blade from its place on the vanity. He shaved quickly, one smooth swipe of the razor after another, rinsing the blade periodically. When he was sure all the stubble had been removed, he splashed his face with cold water and patted it dry with the hand towel that hung just above the light switch. He took a deep breath and blew it out slowly, his hands trembling in anticipation.

After a few contemplative moments, he opened the drawer and beamed at the sight of its contents. Pallets upon pallets of eyeshadow and blush. Tubes of lipstick, bottles of foundation, compacts of powder, bronzer, and contour, all unopened. His face lit up as he took a tube of BB cream in his hands and broke the seal. He squeezed a small amount onto his finger, rubbed it on the back of his hand to warm it up, then dotted it all over his face. He blended it in with a stippling brush until his skin looked flawless. Next, he applied the contour, doing his best to remember the techniques he'd seen on internet how-tos. "Blend, blend, blend." he reminded himself. He then turned his face up in an exaggerated smile, brushing on the soft-pink blush to the apples of his cheeks and eye-lids. He used transparent powder to set before he turned his attention to his eyes. He lined them in deep black before applying mascara and false lashes. Finally, he carefully spread the blood-red lipstick to his full lips then went over them with a clear gloss.

"Almost," he breathed, closing the makeup drawer and opening the medicine cabinet. He'd taken out the shelves and added hooks, allowing him to easily store his many hair extensions. He separated his hair, tying most of it up before clipping in the first extension. He repeated the process until he was happy with the length and fullness. He then added waves with setting spray and a curling iron. He tousled his hair until he was satisfied that he had a natural, "beachy" look.

He stared at himself in the mirror, puckering his lips and tilting his head in different poses. This was it. *This* was who he'd always been meant to be. Hart was over. Dead. He had ceased to be. From now on, there was only Hartley.

"There you are, you beautiful bitch."

Chapter 32

Wendy left Gabriel in bed while she went to pick up a fast-food breakfast; sausage biscuits, hash browns, and apple pie. She had food at her apartment, but she needed an excuse to get some fresh air, the short walk guaranteed to clear her head. She had agreed to help Gabriel without giving it much thought at all. How could she refuse her? She was talking about guarding the *Gate to Heaven*. That wasn't something she could just ignore. Still, it was risky and she could be putting herself in more danger than she realized. She went over the checklist of things she'd need for the spell: Amethyst, Goofer Dust mixed with dirt from her grandmother's grave and a few other things, black, blue, and red candles. She felt like she was forgetting something, but what? Hopefully, it'd come to her once she got some food in her stomach.

Gabriel was still sleeping when she got home. She watched her for a second before deciding that was probably creepy and went to the desk where the cat's eye necklace remained. She debated with herself whether or not to use it, activating her great-aunt's magic and taking it into herself. On one hand, the more power the better. On the other, there was no telling what Grace's magic would do to her. It was strong. She could feel it from across the room. It would take time for her to learn to control it...time they didn't have. No. It was too much of a gamble. She'd leave the amulet where it was. At least, for now. She was confident she could do the spell on her own, no assistance required. As she took the food from its bag and set cans of soda on the table, she hoped she wouldn't regret her decision.

"Hey," Gabriel greeted, sauntering into the kitchen wearing nothing but a tee-shirt. "Yay, food!" She kissed Wendy's cheek and sat down, curling her legs underneath her and shoving a bite of biscuit into her mouth. "You have everything you need?"

"Yeah, my duffel's already packed." She pointed to her bag by the door.

"So prepared."

"Like a boy scout."

"Are you sure you want to do this? It's gonna be hella dangerous."

"I'm sure. I thought about it on the way to get breakfast. What kind of person would I be if I said 'no' to protecting *Heaven*? I mean, really."

"With the threat of getting shot or blown up looming, I'd say 'normal'."

"I'm not normal, though," she smirked.

"Join the club, sister."

They clinked soda cans and drank, their smiles fading as Gabriel held Wendy's hand, kissing the back of it and sighing heavily. "I won't let anything happen to you."

She shook her head. "I don't think you can promise that."

"*Okay*, I promise that if something *does* happen to you, I'll do everything I can to fix it and then take revenge on the dumb son of a bitch that dare lay a hand on you."

She giggled. "I don't doubt that for a second."

They finished eating and moved to the couch, not having to leave for the airport for several hours.

"So, who else is coming? What other angels can I expect to meet today?"

"Lucifer will be there. He's instrumental. He can fly, so we need him to--"

Her jaw dropped. "He can *fly*?"

"Oh, yeah. He'll no doubt whine all the way there about how slow planes are in comparison. Now, he gets a little murdery sometimes, but as long as you don't say anything overtly racist, he won't--"

She chuckled. "Murdery?"

Gabriel shrugged. "Uriel will be there. She likes to be called 'Valerie'. She gets psychic visions sometimes. Kind of judgemental, but funny."

"Not to be a dick, but, how is that helpful in a war?"

"Fiery sword."

She raised her eyebrows. "Oh."

"Then, there's Barachiel, human name Wyatt. His son just died, so be nice."

"Oh, God, that's awful. Wait, angels can have kids?"

"No, not usually."

"Uh, huh. And what's his deal?"

"Protector of Humanity, lightning powers. Then there's his girlfriend."

"I thought you said the angels were like siblings. Oh, gross."

Gabriel erupted in laughter. "No, no. His girlfriend's not one of us. She's a vampire. *Queen* vampire. She's letting us borrow her army to fight off the golem."

"Queen?"

"First of her kind."

They were quiet for a while, the upcoming battle feeling more real as it grew closer. Wendy tapped her bottom lip with her finger. "Is it weird that I'm starting to get excited? Like, giddy, even?"

"Yeah, kind of."

They laughed as Wendy climbed into Gabriel's lap, pinning her to the back of the couch and kissing her playfully. "Do you think we have time to..." She let her voice trail off.

"Oh, we will *make* time."

Valerie decided to get one more practice in before leaving for Iraq, flourishing her sword and moving about the roof of Gabriel's building as if in a choreographed dance. The more she worked with the sword, the more it felt like a part of her, an extension of her arm. It seemed lighter and less cumbersome, easier to control. Once she'd accepted it as hers, once she'd finally fully accepted who she was, the movements came to her like second nature. She was Uriel, Regent of the Sun, Flame of God, Archangel of Salvation. She *would* defend the Gate and cut down any ghoul or goblin that got in her way. Not that she wanted to do it. She couldn't wait for this day to be over. She hadn't gotten much sleep the night before. She'd been too anxious. This wasn't one little-girl-wearing psycho terrorizing frat houses. That had been bad enough. This was an army of freaks, all with two things on their minds: blowing the Gate to shit and slaughtering anyone trying to protect it. She was *not* looking forward to it.

"I see your training has come along nicely." Lucifer leaned against the stone wall next to the door. "Not as well as if you'd let me assist you, but all in all, not too shabby. Pity you have no practical experience."

"I remember enough."

"Do you?" He pulled a sword of his own out from behind him and rushed toward her, raising it above his head and bringing it down hard on her awaiting blade. "Good instincts, sister. Now, let us see how skilled you are when your opponent isn't thin air." He swung again, meeting her sword with a sharp clank. Over and over again he swung at her and over and over again, she deflected. "You seem to have nearly mastered the art of defense. I'm almost impressed." He kept pushing her, switching up his attacks, keeping her on her toes. "Good," he sneered. "Very good, indeed. Now, take an offensive stance."

"What?"

He struck her blade once more. "Come for me."

"I don't--"

He swung again, the force of the blow nearly knocking her down. She righted herself and stared him down, cracking her neck and lifting her blade. "Boy, you have done it now." She flew forward, crashing her sword into his, one furious swing after another sending him reeling back, laughing as he held her off.

"Excellent! Look how far you've come, Uriel. Dare I say, I'm quite proud of you."

She threw her sword down again, this time allowing it to burst into white-hot flame as it met Lucifer's. His eyes grew wide and he scurried backward, putting some distance between himself and the blaze.

"Are you mad?" he admonished, throwing down his sword and folding his arms like a disappointed father.

The flame went out and she sheathed her weapon. "What?"

"Are you trying to kill me just as we're about to go into battle? You do realize the rest of you will *not* be victorious without my help."

"I'm not trying to-- hold up. I thought *nothing* could kill you. God's strongest and whatnot."

"You wield *Holy Fire*. That can kill *anything*. Well, *nearly* anything."

"Really?" she smirked. "That is very interesting information. Good to know. *Good to know.*"

"Don't go getting all high and mighty, sister. You're still incredibly undisciplined and lack the proper footwork to--"

"Why do you continue to hassle me?"

"*I'm helping you.* You may have bested a single golem, but you've never come up against *ten thousand* of them, not even in your true form. You have no idea the danger you're in. While I have every confidence that we will prevail, I am *not* certain that you and the others will make it out of the desert with your heads still attached. Barachiel is the only one of you that can survive such a fate as beheading and *that's* assuming his vampire doesn't get herself killed. You must be prepared."

"Aww, Lucifer. Are you saying you care about me? You gettin' soft?"

He rolled his eyes and let out a sigh of derision.

"Fine. You were helping. But I'm good. Don't you worry your pretty little head."

He growled under his breath.

She giggled. "All right, come on. Let's get something to eat before we go."

"As long as it's real food."

"So, nothing from downstairs."

"Definitely not."

"You should get some sleep," Wyatt said, adjusting his pillow as Allydia rolled back to her side of the bed.

"I'll sleep on the plane. Until we leave, I will cherish you."

His dark eyes lingered on her face as she smiled at him. He tucked her hair behind her ear, sending shivers down her spine, the gentleness of his touch like catnip. "I could stare at you all day."

"And I you," she purred.

"We will have to get out of bed, eventually."

"Yes, *eventually*."

As he looked at her, his thoughts turned to the upcoming battle. "How dangerous will this be for you?"

"Mild to moderate."

"I'm serious. Are you worried?"

"No."

"No?"

"I've come against worse and won."

"Worse than an army of unkillable monsters?"

"They're not unkillable to things like me. All one need do is remove the head. My soldiers and I can do that with one hand tied behind our backs. In fact, on one occasion, I had to do just that. I had been vacationing in Santorini, I think it was around the end of the nineteenth century. Beginning of the twentieth? I had gotten a tad reckless, exposed myself. The locals discovered what I was and before I knew it, they had me strapped to a stake. They were cocky, so sure of their vampire hunting abilities. The smug looks on their faces made my blood boil even before the fire was set. The man with the torch made the mistake of getting just a little too close--"

"I feel like I don't want to hear the rest of that story."

"Oh. Then, perhaps you'd like me to tell you about the time I aided the Ottoman Empire in taking down one of my own? It was December 1476. He'd been drawing attention to himself for *years* and the number of dead he left as trophies, just out in the open, was a *clear* violation of my laws. I could not abide it. So, I found him in Bucharest--"

Wyatt shook his head, indicating that he didn't want to hear *that* story, either.

"The Crusades?"

"No."

"Pompeii?"

"Uh, uh."

"Battling the Neph--" She stopped herself.

He gave her a stern look of warning.

"Of course," she said, touching his cheek. "My point is, you don't have to worry about me. I've been taking care of myself for a very long time."

"I know that, but it doesn't change the way I feel."

"And, how do you feel?"

He brought her hand to his lips and closed his eyes, taking in the sweet scent of the perfume she had made from the gardenias that grew in her rooftop garden. It rose from her wrist and enveloped his senses with nearly the same intoxicating quality as her pheromones. His hunger for her again began to build as she moved closer. His mind went foggy as she brushed his chin with her fingertips.

"Wyatt, how do you feel?"

He struggled to speak, her pheromones taking hold. He ran his hand over her body, starting at her neck and gliding his fingers down. "Are you tired?"

"Almost," she breathed, her cheeks flushed and her skin tingling. Her eyes bore into his, the intensity between them growing. "I want you to exhaust me."

Unable to hold back, he threw himself on top of her, spreading her legs wide and entering with more force than usual. She drew in a sharp breath as he buried his face in her hair and kissed her neck, her hands sliding down his back. She writhed against him, hushed moans escaping her lips as her body quaked. All thoughts of the upcoming conflict and inevitable bloodshed fled their minds. At that moment, there was only this room, this bed, and each other. Nothing else mattered.

Chapter 33

Spade and his men had just made camp in the Iraqi desert, taking time to rest before the impending battle. The soldiers moved like robots, never speaking and doing as they were told with efficiency. If things continued to run this smoothly, they'd have their target destroyed and be on their way home by lunch. He didn't want to get too arrogant, though. The scout he'd sent to the apartment of the woman whose clothes he'd put a tracker on had never returned, most likely meaning that he'd been killed. In war, things can go sideways at the drop of a hat. Best not to get too comfortable.

In the distance, he spotted a convoy of pickup trucks heading toward the camp. As they drew closer, he could see the machine guns mounted on them with men in the beds at the ready. Typical Islamic extremist fighters. He'd dealt with these groups dozens of times over the years and prepared himself to talk them down, hoping to avoid a conflict.

The trucks stopped and one man walked toward him, apparently the speaker for the group. He held a rifle but didn't point it at him. Instead, he looked him over, distrust and contempt evident in his eyes. "What are you doing here?" he asked, more of an accusation than a question.

"We've gotten word that a neo-Nazi outfit is here looking to destroy Muslim cultural sites," Spade lied, feeding him the same story he'd told authorities when he'd arrived. "We're here to apprehend them and take them back to the States for prosecution."

The man was clearly skeptical.

"Have you seen this man?" Spade pulled a picture from his pocket and showed it to him. It was of the wounded soldier that hadn't returned from the scouting mission. "We believe he's the ringleader of the operation. Goes by 'Charlie'."

The man shook his head after examining the photo.

"All right, well, we'll be here for a few hours to grab some shut-eye then we'll be out of your hair."

"No," the man insisted. "You will leave now." He raised his hand, signaling the others. They began knocking things over and using knives to tear at the tents the soldiers were sleeping in.

Spade frowned. "We don't want any trouble."

"But, you have found it. We will take your weapons and tanks and leave you to die. That will teach your government to interfere in matters that don't concern them. If there *are* people trying to destroy our history, *we* will handle them, our way."

The commotion woke the soldiers who stumbled out of the tents, their eyes distant. They stood quietly, waiting for orders, unable to make a move without instruction. Thousands of them gathered, silent as the extremists readied their weapons.

"Are you sure you want to die?" Spade asked the leader.

The man scoffed. "It is *you* who wi--"

Spade pulled his side-arm and shot the man in the forehead. "Kill them!"

The soldiers leaped into action, shooting, stabbing, and strangling everyone in the opposition. As they, too, were injured, they kept attacking, ignoring their own bullet wounds. Spade ducked behind an LUV and watched enthusiastically as his men took out the enemy without hesitation. They had no fear, no survival instinct, and seemed incapable of feeling pain. They were murdering machines devoid of emotion or thought. They had a singular goal: to carry out their Commander's orders. Perfect soldiers. "Thank you, Lilith," Spade whispered.

When the dust settled and the last of the extremists was dead, he called to his men, "At ease!" They stopped in their tracks. After assessing the damage, he gave the next order. "Put the bodies in the trucks and confiscate the weapons." The men did as they were told, carrying two corpses at a time to the pickups and throwing them in the beds. They gathered the guns and laid them in a pile at Spade's feet. "Pack up. Once we get moving, we'll IED those sons of bitches." The soldiers got to work with no complaints, some bleeding from the chest, a few spilling blood and brain matter from gaping head wounds. He watched in awe as they labored, the guilt of stripping them of their humanity replaced by excitement. He was confident now that they would have no problem completing their mission and fulfilling his duty to his employer. From there, the sky was the limit. With an army of unkillable soldiers, his business would become even more profitable. Since they were basically robots, they would never need to go home. He may even get away with not paying them. He felt invigorated and was actually looking forward to the next battle.

The men filled the LUV's and DPV's after setting the bombs and as they drove away, the timer ticked down. The last vehicle was less than half a mile away when the timer reached zero, setting off a chain of explosions so loud, Spade worried that more hostiles would show up, causing another conflict. As he looked over the three soldiers in the vehicle with him, stone-faced and diligent, he smiled and said to himself, "Let them come."

Chapter 34

"Who's she talking to?" Wyatt asked, watching Gabriel pace around the back of the plane as he absentmindedly stroked Allydia's hair, her head in his lap as she slept.

"The president of Iraq," Lucifer answered, sitting across from him and next to Wendy. "The area needs to be evacuated."

"How does she plan on getting him to do that?"

"Bribery, I imagine."

"Is she all right?" Wendy wondered, looking at Allydia's motionless face.

"She's fine," Wyatt insisted.

"It doesn't look like she's breathing."

"That's because she's a vampire," Lucifer informed her.

"Well, sure." She looked her over, head tilted and eyebrows furrowed.

"What?" Wyatt scowled.

"Nothing, I just didn't think they'd be so *hot*. I had this whole pale, sunken in cheeks, Nosferatu picture in my head. Also, I'm a little surprised they don't sleep in coffins."

Lucifer chuckled. "I like this one."

"We should *all* be getting some sleep," Valerie interjected from across the aisle. "Thousands of what-the-fucks aren't gonna kill *themselves* and I don't know about you, but I want to be alert when I get to head-chopping."

Wendy smiled. "You're amazing."

"All right, kids," Gabriel said, sitting across from Valerie and putting her phone in her bag. "He's evacuating a fifty-mile radius. Should be plenty to prevent any civilian casualties."

"How much did that cost you?" Lucifer inquired.

"Two million."

"Holy crap!" Wendy gasped.

"It's all right, love," Lucifer told her. "My sister has nearly limitless funds. Inherited wealth, you understand. She didn't tell you?"

She shook her head.

Gabriel shot him a look. "It's not important."

"Of course not," he smirked. "But, seeing as how you've yet to tell any of us how exactly you came to acquire your family fortune, one can't help but wonder."

"I didn't kill my parents, dick."

"No, I wouldn't think so. But, *something* happened to them and your refusal to discuss it must mean that their deaths weren't purely natural."

Wyatt stared him down. "Do I have to get up?"

Lucifer raised his eyebrow.

"Can we focus?" Valerie snapped. "You all know we're heading into a war zone, right? We're about to be knee-deep in zombie-soldiers shooting at us, armed with nothing but a sword, some crystals, fireworks, and a bunch of blood-suckers who, for the life of me, I can't figure out why they'd be helping us. Exactly why in the ever-loving fuck are you bickering right now?"

The group was silent for a moment before Lucifer snorted. "They're not 'zombies'. They're *alive*, just--"

"Are you *fucking* kidding me?"

"Okay, there's obviously some tension here, so," Wendy waved her hand at them. "Somnus."

Wyatt, Valerie, and Lucifer fell unconscious as Gabriel beamed. "You're the best thing ever."

"Really?" she flirted, gliding across the aisle and into the seat next to her. "You wanna maybe," she slid her hand up Gabriel's thigh. "Spend some quality time?"

"They could wake up."

"Not for eight solid hours. The plane could burst into flames, crash into the ocean. We could all get eaten by sharks. They'd sleep right through it. There are about ten hours left on this flight. That gives them all kinds of time to wake up, eat and prepare themselves."

"Eat?"

She pointed to her duffel in the overhead compartment. "I brought snacks."

Gabriel grabbed her face and grinned. "Damn it, you *are* the best." She kissed her and began fiddling with her belt buckle. "What's this pants crap?"

They woke up to the sound of individual chip bags being placed in front of them on treys. Bottles of water and sandwiches accompanied them. "It's crunchy peanut butter with strawberry jam because that's my favorite," Wendy informed them. "I also have chocolates for dessert."

"Well, aren't you two perfect for each other?" Lucifer quipped. "Shared unhealthy eating habits as well as a penchant for using your powers against the rest of us."

"I'm sorry," she claimed. "But you were all too rowdy. Snapping at each other, being rude. Valerie was right, you needed a nap."

"Who are you?" Allydia asked, having fallen asleep before Wendy had boarded the plane.

"Gabriel's new playmate," Lucifer told her.

"Girlfriend," Gabriel corrected.

"Really?" Allydia asked. "I didn't think you were capable of monogamy, Messenger. Are you finding it difficult?"

"No."

"It's okay if you are," Wendy assured her. "Allydia, I made a sandwich for you, too, but Gabriel just told me you can't eat regular food."

"That's all right, I brought my own." She pulled a blood bag from the cooler next to her and began to drink.

Wyatt averted his eyes. "Still not used to that."

"Thanks for the food," Valerie said through a mouthful of chips. "But, don't fuck with me like that again."

"Cross my heart," Wendy giggled.

They ate in silence for the next several minutes, all of them anxious about the upcoming battle. All except

Wyatt, who no longer *wanted* to die, but wasn't one hundred percent against it, either.

The jet landed in the middle of the desert, as per Gabriel's instructions. The planes carrying the army of vampires were already there and as Allydia headed toward the door to leave, she turned to address Lucifer. "Would you mind?"

"Not at all." He exited first and looked up to the midday sky. He took a deep breath and as he exhaled, the sky became overcast with thick, dark clouds. Now safe from the sun's radiation, Allydia went to join her general and assemble her soldiers.

"Neat," Wendy approved as she and Gabriel stepped onto the sand.

"You're not the only one with tricks up their sleeves."

"You ready for this?" Valerie asked as she and Wyatt walked to meet the others.

"Not at all," he admitted.

"Yeah, me, neither."

They made the short hike to the ruins of ancient Babylon. As they drew closer, the ground became greener. There were palm trees and shrubbery all fed by the Euphrates River.

"You can set up right here," Gabriel told Wendy, who nodded and began placing large amethysts in a circle.

"So, this is Babylon," she said. "Pretty."

"It's buried a few miles down. Is that an issue?"

"Not as long as I'm right on top of it." She poured the Goofer Dust around the stones and set candles in between. "Crap in a hat!"

"What?"

"I didn't bring a lighter. I knew I was forgetting something."

Gabriel chuckled. "Girl, I got you." She waved her hand, lighting all the candles at once.

"Goddamn, you are *handy*."

"And here come the vampires," Valerie groaned, leaning on her sword. The others turned to see thousands of the creatures, somehow their allies, headed toward them, Allydia and another woman in the lead.

"They really *will* do anything she asks," Wyatt said.

"You just figuring that out now?" Gabriel asked.

"I told you," Lucifer groused. "They worship her. They revere her as a mother, savior, judge, jury, and executioner. She's a god to them. It's disgusting."

"Don't start," Gabriel warned.

In the distance, they could see them coming; the military vehicles approached like a herd of wild horses, loud and fast. Valerie lifted her sword, igniting it in a burst of flames. Wyatt began gathering energy from the blackened sky and Lucifer clenched his fists.

Wendy got on her knees in the center of the circle and began to chant, "Praesidio in loco isto."

"Get ready, kids," Gabriel said, stepping forward. "Shit's about to get dicey."

Chapter 35

Allydia stopped and faced her soldiers, an army of the undead, ready to kill or be killed for their Queen. They halted and knelt before her as she began to address them, none of them looking her in the eyes.

"My finest warriors, you humble me with your willingness to fight. You honor me with your sacrifice. I am proud beyond words to call you my children. Some of you may die here today, far from home and for a cause you may not see as your own. Take solace in the fact that what you do here is just and I am grateful for your contribution. Take pride in knowing that until your dying day, you served your Queen well and you will not be forgotten."

The crowd cheered, standing as she turned away. "Assume your positions!" Phindi called.

Lucifer stepped away from his siblings to speak into Allydia's ear as she approached. "If anything happens to my brother, I will hold you personally responsible."

"If anything happens to your brother, I will rip out my own heart with my bare hands."

As a swarm of drones flew overhead, Lucifer rocketed up to meet them, swatting them into each other, exploding them in the sky above. When the last craft was disabled, he moved on to the vehicles, pouncing on them and lifting them up before dropping them on the enemy soldiers below. He was a one-man army, plowing through LUV's, tanks, and DPV's. All that was left were the golem themselves, which he was useless against in his host body. He rejoined the others as Wyatt pulled bolts of white-hot lightning from the clouds and threw them into the crowd. The army of monsters was stunned, but got up and kept coming.

"Well, that's unsettling," he complained.

"Stay behind me," Allydia instructed.

"I can take care of myself."

"Nothing living can harm them. If they get close, I'm the only one here that can protect you."

"Ready!" they heard Phindi shout. The vampires were in formation, stationed between the Gate and the golem. As the enemy got closer, the vampire general raised her hand. Her soldiers nearly vibrated with excitement, hungry for the fight that was to come. "Remember, if you can't get their heads off, just the bottom lip will do!" The general dropped her arm. "Attack!"

The vampires raced to the opposition, hacking off heads with swords as bullets began to fly. Vampires carrying no weapons flung themselves on enemy combatants like spider monkeys, tearing the bottom lips from their vacant faces and watching in amazement when they fell.

"How is that killing them?" Wyatt wondered.

Lucifer folded his arms. "They've been marked with the Word of God, enslaving them to the one whose blood was used in the ritual. One of Lilith's spells. Always with the blood magic, that one. She was obsessed with trading one life for another. Or many. Isn't that right, Your Majesty?"

Allydia shot him a look.

"The Word of God?" Wyatt asked.

Lucifer nodded. "One of His names. Considered sacred by humans of certain religions, though it matters little to Him what people choose to call Him. Imagine if the bacteria in your gut had a name for you. Would you mind?"

Suddenly, an explosion boomed above them, the grenade crashing into the invisible wall Wendy's protection spell had put in place. It was hit with another and another and Wendy's arms began to shake as she chanted louder, the shield weakening with every blow.

The fighting between the two armies continued. Vampires were slaughtered en masse with bullets through the heart. Golem were torn to shreds by vengeful vampires. The battle drew closer to the Gate and as the wall began to thin, a stray bullet got through, hitting

Wendy in her liver. She bled out and as the light from her stormy eyes faded, the wall dissolved, leaving the Gate and the siblings vulnerable.

"Wendy!" Gabriel cried, rushing to her girlfriend's side. She pulled the bullet from her body with her mind and placed her hands on the wound. Her skin glowed and the wound slowly healed, but her eyes remained closed. "Wake up. Please, wake up." Gabriel's heart pounded in her ears and her mind raced. She thought she might hyperventilate. "Lucifer,"

"Yes, sister?" he answered, crouching next to her.

She looked at him, the fear in her eyes unsettling him. He'd never seen her afraid. She choked back tears, her voice shaky as she spoke. "I think I'm in love with her."

"Oh, fuck this shit," Valerie blurted, stepping outside the circle and swinging her flame-engulfed sword, lopping the heads off every golem she came across. Wyatt, too, stepped away from the group, throwing balls of lightning at the soldiers as they swarmed.

"Remember what I said," Lucifer warned, jumping up and grabbing Allydia by the arm.

She shot back, "Wyatt is the most important thing to me in this world. I will not fail him." She went after her beloved, planting herself between him and the monsters.

Horror covered the face of one of the vampires, seeing his Queen put a human before her own kind, before her own life, filling him with anger and disgust. He ran off, deserting her and her cause, unwilling to risk himself for a Queen whose heart was not fully with him and his people.

"Please be okay," Gabriel whispered as she put her ear to Wendy's heart. She couldn't hear over the sounds of the battlefield. She pressed harder but nothing. She put her fingers to her wrist to feel for a pulse. It was there. Faint, but there. After a few seconds, it got stronger and she opened her eyes.

"You were right, dying is *really* unpleasant."

"Are you okay?" Gabriel fretted.

"I think so," she said, struggling to stand.

"Stay here. Get the spell back up if you can."

"Where are you going?"

"To fight," she said, marching toward the action. "I'm in a mood." She raised her hands, determination and rage coloring her face. As she concentrated, the remaining golem burst into flames. It didn't kill them. They carried on, shooting and fending off vampires. Eventually, the flames went out, Gabriel being alive rendering her powers all but useless against them.

"It was you," Wyatt realized. "In the theater with Lilith's demons. *You* killed those people."

"Lecture me about it later." Just then, Spade came barreling through the crowd, pistol drawn, a smug grin plastered on his five o'clock shadow-covered face.

"We meet again," he smirked, pulling the trigger and shooting her twice in the stomach.

Allydia held Wyatt back as he tried to rush him. "She will heal."

"And you," Spade scoffed, approaching Lucifer. "Flying. Impressive. Let's see if you can survive a straight shot to the temple."

As he pointed the gun at Lucifer's face, the shot ringing out and the bullet being released, they heard Wendy cry out, "Subsisto!" The bullet stopped in mid-air and fell to the ground between the two men. Lucifer sneered.

"How is that possible?!" Spade spat.

"He's the one that can't be hurt by supernatural creatures?" Wendy asked.

Lucifer nodded.

"Interesting spell. My grandmother told me about a witch who could work it, back in the day. Not easy."

Spade shot again, and again, while Wendy easily stopped the bullets. "What are you people?!"

"There's no way to straight remove it," Wendy continued. "All you can do is," She held her hand out, palm facing him, and flicked her wrist, pointing her fingers toward herself. "Transuerso."

"What did you do?" Spade demanded.

Lucifer stepped toward him, his face twisted in an evil grin. He slapped him and laughed. "She shifted the warding to herself. I knew a Tituban witch would come in handy. A lesson for you, Wendy. My Father will occasionally put people in our lives for a purpose. As for you, Mr. Spade, sadly, your time here has passed."

The general tried to run, but Lucifer snatched him by the hair. "A coward on top of everything else? Shameful." He threw him to the ground.

"Lucifer," Gabriel called, clutching her bleeding gut, unable to move from where she'd fallen as she healed.

He gave her a sideways glance in acknowledgment.

Through heavy breaths, she all but ordered him, "Make it hurt."

He smiled again and returned his gaze to the fallen general. "As you wish, sister." He tore off Spade's right arm first, assuring he wouldn't be firing his gun again. He plucked off the other, then his legs, reveling in the savagery of it. He was nearly laughing as blood sprayed in all directions.

Spade howled, the pain so intense it brought tears to his eyes. "My employer won't stop!" he swore. "He'll find another way! He *will* destroy this place!"

Gabriel walked up, inspecting the holes in her shirt. She sighed and stood over him, looking him in the eye. "You let *me* worry about Cain."

Lucifer plunged his hand into Spade's gut, pulling out intestines like a magician pulling scarves from his sleeve. The man convulsed, blood sputtering from his mouth. He went ghostly white, his eyes glazing over. Finally, he stopped moving, the life leaving him. When he was dead, the last of the golem fell, their lives having been intertwined with his. The battle was over.

Chapter 36

Only nine hundred vampires remained. They lined up their fallen and paid their respects, Allydia and Phindi watching as they said goodbye.

"Africa," the Queen told her general. "The entire continent. And the Middle East. They're yours now."

"Your Majesty?"

"Duchess Phindi, Ruler of The Old World's, yours *and* mine. Second only to me, you answer to none of my Governors anywhere in the world."

"That is too great of an honor, my Queen."

"You deserve it. You've proven yourself loyal and worthy. You're strong. A leader."

"I am humbled. It is a privilege."

"It's what you've earned." She held back the urge to shed tears as she watched her people mourn. "Do you know how old I am?"

"You are the first of our kind. I assume you must be thousands of years old."

"Yes. Almost as old as humanity itself. I've seen wars, famine, and plague. I've seen the rise and fall of nations and empires. Through it all, I've maintained our way of life. *Us*, the vampiric race. I've kept us out of human affairs, for the most part, separating us from their petty skirmishes. But, *this*...I couldn't ignore this."

"May I ask why, my Queen?"

"The people I traveled with, you saw what they can do?"

"The man that wields lightning as a weapon? The woman that heals herself from death?"

Allydia nodded. "They're not *strictly* human. They're something else, something older. It devastates me to see my people die and more to see the ones that did not suffer the loss. But, these people speak for something higher. I could not refuse them."

"Higher? What could be higher than *you*, my Queen?"

"Only one thing."

She was taken aback. "You speak of a Creator?"

"We called Him 'Elohim'. I thought my father had invented Him. An easy explanation for the things in life he couldn't account for. I only believed him after my stepmother made me this."

"You talk of *God*."

She nodded.

"I don't know what to say."

"You'll say nothing. I trust only *you* with this."

"Why not tell the others? Forgive me, my Queen, but this is--"

"The ability to believe what one wishes without actually *knowing* keeps people sane," she told her. "I'm old enough to remember a time when God spoke directly to humans. They took His words out of context, bastardized His commands, killed each other for the right to call themselves His. The only true difference between us and the humans is that we feel more deeply. Imagine the zealotry that could emerge, the harm they could do to each other. Better God remain a vague idea than something tangible to be acquired like love or fear. You will keep this to yourself, yes? My faith in you has not been misplaced?"

"Of course, Your Majesty. I serve at your pleasure. And...do you serve God?"

She laughed. "I serve no one. But I do respect Him."

The vampires boarded the planes, leaving their comrades where they lay. Allydia joined them and they took off, heading quickly back to the States.

Once she was sure the vampires were out of sight range, Gabriel waved her hand at the makeshift memorial, then at the pile of golem, setting ablaze the thousands of bodies, Spade's mangled corpse thrown in with his soldiers, his dead eyes seeming to stare her down as they burned.

Back on the jet, Valerie curled up in a window seat and closed her eyes. "Hey, witch, any chance of getting another one of those power naps?"

Wendy giggled. "I thought you said--"

"Girl, I know what I said, but I'm tired as hell."

"All right, then. Somnus."

Valerie passed out, a light snore the only sound she made for the rest of the trip.

"So, problem solved?" Lucifer asked.

"For now," Gabriel told him.

"Wonderful," he rejoiced. "I should like to visit a certain bartender. It's been some time since--"

"I am begging you not to finish that sentence."

Wendy took her arm and led her to the back of the plane, out of her brother's view.

The two men sat quietly for a time until Wyatt's curiosity got the better of him. "You were willing to take the fall for what I did to Will. Why?"

Lucifer raised his eyebrows and sat back in his seat. "Your personality is quite volatile. You aren't always rational. I thought the knowledge of what you'd done would torment you, push you over the edge. I was right."

"I could have killed you."

He laughed. "You could have *what*? At *full power,* you couldn't kill me, much less in this meat puppet you're wearing."

"Still,"

"You already weren't very fond of me. Hating me would have been easy and I would have allowed it to spare your precious human emotions."

"Why?"

"Because that's what brothers do."

After a long silence, Wyatt spoke again. "You're God's favorite."

"So they say."

"So you know Him, what He's like?"

"If memory serves."

Wyatt let out a breath and looked into his brother's eyes. "Does He hate me?"

"What? Of course not. He doesn't hate anyone, especially His Protector of Humanity. You're special to Him, as am I and Gabriel and--"

"Did I do something to make Him angry? Did I offend Him somehow?"

He snickered. "Contrary to social media's comments sections, our Father isn't offended by much of anything."

"Then, why would He allow this? I know He's asleep or whatever, but Gabriel told me He made it *impossible*, so how did it happen? *Why* did it happen? Why would He give me a son only to turn around and take him away from me?"

Lucifer didn't know how to answer that, but he'd brought up a good point. "I don't know, brother."

Wyatt wiped away a stray tear. "It's not right."

"No," he agreed. "No, I don't believe it is."

Chapter 37

Gabriel watched the girl playing in the front yard. Her mother was inside, grief-stricken, leaving the child alone as not to burden her with her tears.

"Jenny," Gabriel said as she approached. The girl looked up and Gabriel studied her; she seemed unafraid, naively trusting. She took her hand and urged her to sit on the ground next to her, which she did. "I'm sorry about your dad. He loved you very much. He prayed every day that you'd get better. That's why I'm here. To make you better."

The girl didn't seem to understand. She continued playing with the blocks, all but ignoring the stranger's presence.

"I'm gonna touch your head now," Gabriel warned. "It'll feel weird for a second while I repair some connections in your brain, but when it's over, you'll be good as new, okay? Here I go." She placed her hands on the girl's temples, lighting up the skin on her face. Her eyes grew wide and she dropped the toys, the light stinging sensations surprising her. Her eyes rolled back and her bottom lip quivered as every vein in her face became visible. After a few moments of concentration, Gabriel took her hands away, satisfied with the healing. "How do you feel?"

The girl looked at her, directly this time, shock and gratitude in her eyes. "Ah," she croaked. "I feel like I'm here. Really *here*. What are you?"

"Angel. Don't tell anyone, though. They'll think you're crazy. Just tell your mom you hit your head. She won't question it. They'll call it 'a miracle'."

She nodded.

"I'm gonna go before someone sees me. Remember," she covered her lips with her finger as if to say, 'shh'. The girl nodded again.

As Gabriel stood and walked away, she could hear the girl yell, "Mom! Mom!" Once across the street, she turned to look as the woman rushed outside and fell to her knees, tears spilling down her already puffy cheeks. The two embraced and Gabriel left, her guilt over Spade fading. He may have been an evil piece of shit, but he *was* human. Healing his daughter seemed like a good enough way to right things. Hopefully, when she saw her Father again, He wouldn't be too terribly upset with her.

Chapter 38

Hattie placed a log on the fire. The Highlands could feel chilly, even in the summer, especially in old stone buildings like this one.

The man struggled to free himself, but she'd tied the ropes tight around him and the chair he sat on. He wasn't going anywhere. Screams from the next room drowned out his muffled pleas as she released the valve on his IV, allowing his blood to flow into the awaiting glass. Tears fell from his eyes as she replaced the valve.

"Stop complaining," she dismissed. "I already told you I'm not going to kill you. When you've lost so much blood, you'll pass out, I'll drop you at the pub and the barmaid will call a doctor. You'll be fine."

He cried through the gag in his mouth.

"Come now, I can't just let her die, can I? It's not as though she's in a condition to feed herself." She patted him on the back and left him there, scurrying to get the fresh blood to her friend before it went cold. "Here we are." She held the glass to Michelle's mouth and she drank, unquenchable thirst driving her nearly to the point of madness. She was drenched in sweat, exhausted, and in pain. The blood helped, but it wasn't enough.

"I need more," Michelle breathed.

"I told you, only so much at a time. If we drain him too quickly--"

"More!" she bellowed.

"All right, all right. Here," she held her wrist out. "Take some of mine. It's not the same, but it'll hold you over until we can tap Callum again."

Michelle's pupils dilated and her fangs grew. She bit down hard into her friend's wrist, greedily taking as much as would come. After a few moments, Hattie yanked her arm away. "That's enough, now." She got the towel from the bowl of water on the nightstand and wiped it over Michelle's forehead. The girl fell back into the pillows, letting the sense of relief wash over, knowing it was only temporary.

"Why?" Michelle whimpered.

"I don't know, dear. We've had this conversation already. I'm not the person to ask. Almost over now."

Another wave of excruciating pain gripped her, this time accompanied by a puddle of blood seeping from her nightgown to the bedsheets. She cried out in anguish as Hattie went to the end of the bed and lifted the gown. "It's time, girl."

"No. I can't. This isn't right."

"Right or not, it's happening. Now, pull yourself together and push!"

The End

The Complete Seventh Day Series

Seraphim
Nephilim
Elohim
Cain
Alukah
Coven
Sinclair

Printed in Great Britain
by Amazon